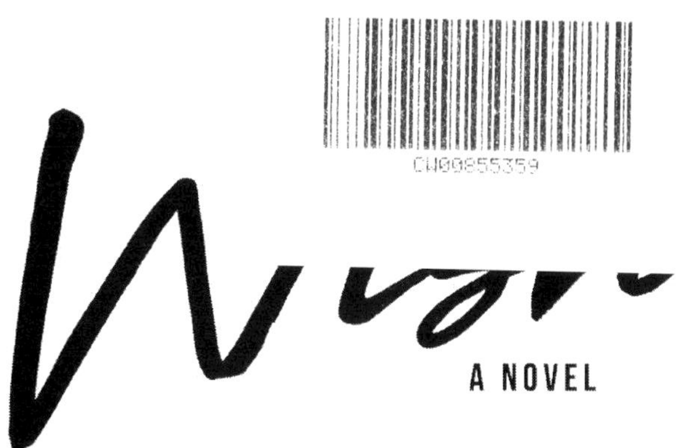

A NOVEL

NEW YORK TIMES BESTSELLING AUTHOR

DEBORAH
BLADON

FIRST ORIGINAL EDITION, JUNE 2018

ISBN-13: 9781987524802
ISBN-10: 1987524802
eBook ISBN: 9781926440514

Book & cover design by Wolf & Eagle Media

www.deborahbladon.com

To Amanda

I could not have done this without you.

Thank you for being there every step of the way.

Here's to fifty more books.

I love you.

Also by Deborah Bladon

THE OBSESSED SERIES
THE EXPOSED SERIES
THE PULSE SERIES
THE VAIN SERIES
THE RUIN SERIES
IMPULSE
SOLO
THE GONE SERIES
FUSE
THE TRACE SERIES
CHANCE
THE EMBER SERIES
THE RISE SERIES
HAZE
SHIVER
TORN
THE HEAT SERIES
MELT
THE TENSE DUET
SWEAT
TROUBLEMAKER
WORTH
HUSH
BARE

Chapter 1

Tilly

I can't look away.

I know that I should. I realize that it's the right thing to do, but my gaze stays locked on the sight that's in front of me.

It's an intricate tattoo that covers the broad left shoulder of a man. The sharp lines of dark ink dip down to curl around his muscular bicep.

The ink on his skin isn't the only mesmerizing thing about him. This man is not only tall and dangerously good-looking, but he's hung. As in, the-largest-cock-I've-ever-seen hung.

The stranger in my apartment isn't wearing any clothes. He's completely naked and standing next to the now dead bouquet of flowers that were delivered to me before I boarded a flight to San Francisco five days ago.

His eyes are closed, his phone is in his hand, ear buds are tucked in place, and he's swaying slowly to what must be music I can't hear.

I should walk over to him and tap him on the shoulder, but I can't.

My feet have been planted in this spot, just inside the foyer of my apartment since I got home a few minutes ago.

My roommate, Lisa, wasn't expecting me to come back for another three days.

We don't keep in touch when one of us is out of town. We barely speak when we pass each other in the hallway.

Lisa and I are not friends.

We're roommates; nothing more and nothing less.

She has every right to invite a guy over. We only have one unspoken rule. I don't knock if her bedroom door is closed, and she does the same if mine is shut.

This is the first time I've ever caught a glimpse of one of the men she's sleeping with. It was worth the wait. This man is ridiculously hot.

I have to cross the room so I can get to the hallway that leads to my bedroom. I need to do that without the naked stranger noticing me. The last thing I want is to make small talk with Lisa's lover right now.

I finally pull my gaze away from him to look down at the hardwood floors. I need to think. I know the sight of Lisa's latest is jumbling my thought process. It's understandable though. Who wouldn't have trouble focusing when an incredibly attractive naked man is across the room?

"Matilda?"

I close my eyes when I hear the distinctive rumble of a deep voice. Why does this man's voice have to sound so damn sexy?

I've never corrected Lisa about my name. Matilda Jean Baker is my full name, so my lawyer used it for the rental agreement I had Lisa sign before she moved in. Almost everyone, other than my boss, calls me Tilly.

I admit I like that the naked stranger is calling me Matilda, although I'm shocked Lisa bothered to mention me to him.

My eyes open and I try to focus on the phone in my hand. It's a stall tactic. I'm hesitant to look up again. I've already got a mental image of his body. I doubt I'll ever forget it.

"That's me." I sigh.

I hear his footsteps as he nears me.

Dammit. The naked stranger is almost right in front of me.

"I thought you were going to be in San Francisco until Sunday."

"I came home early," I say evenly.

I eye his bare feet. I know eventually I need to look up, but he's so close now and I don't trust myself not to stare at his dick. From this vantage point, I'll be able to see every vein and how wide the crown is.

"Matilda, are you okay? You're trembling." His hand brushes against my shoulder. "It's freezing outside. Did you come from the airport dressed like that?"

He's one to talk. At least I'm wearing clothes. The ripped jeans and old red college T-shirt I'm wearing did nothing to protect me from the blast of winter weather that arrived while I was gone. When I left last week, it was forty degrees warmer than it is now.

"I'll make some coffee."

My head darts up when he makes that announcement. Who offers to make a pot of coffee at two a.m. when they're wearing nothing and their lover is probably waiting in her bedroom for another round?

My gaze skims over his smooth chest until it lands on the faux fur blanket he's wrapped around his waist. His left hand is resting on his hip, the blanket's edges bunched into his fist.

"I didn't startle you, did I?" He looks down and into my eyes. "It's dark in here. You probably didn't even notice I was standing over there until I said your name."

It's not that dark.

He's unaware that I was staring at him when I first walked in. That means I won't have to awkwardly try and explain to my roommate why I was checking out her nude lover.

At least now he's grabbed the blanket from where it's usually placed over the back of the leather couch. I use that blanket to wrap around myself when I watch my favorite shows in the evening. Now, I'll always think about the fact that it touched his naked body.

I shake that thought from my head. "I should get to bed. It's been a long day for me."

He nods. "I understand. There's nothing better than sleeping in your own bed after a trip."

I reach to pick up my suitcase before I head toward my bedroom. He's wrong. The only thing better than sleeping in my bed after my trip to San Francisco would be sleeping next to him. Although, after seeing him naked, sleep would be the last thing I'd want to do.

"It's been a pleasure meeting you, Matilda," he calls from behind me.

The pleasure is all mine. It's technically all Lisa's. She's the one who gets to enjoy what I just saw.

With any luck, I won't hear the two of them together. After the week I just had, the last thing I need is a reminder that there are men in the world who know how to a fuck a woman raw.

I have no doubt that the naked stranger in my living room is one of them.

Chapter 2

Tilly

"Pay attention, Frannie," I scold my identical twin sister as I adjust my phone in my hand until my face comes into full view of the camera. I hate video chatting, but it's one of Frannie's favorite things to do. She tells me she misses my face. I tell her to look in the mirror and she'll see exactly what I look like. "I need to call Maya. Can we talk later?"

Frannie shakes her head from side-to-side. That sends her long brown hair tumbling over her shoulders. We may be twenty-five-years-old now and live on opposite sides of the country, but we still share the same hairstyle.

One visible difference between us is Frannie almost always has her blue eyes rimmed with a dark liner to make them pop. I opt for a sheer shadow and two layers of mascara.

It's barely past the crack of dawn in San Francisco, but my twin already has her hair styled and her makeup applied, even though the most pressing thing on her schedule today consists of a visit to the zoo with her husband, two daughters, and our parents.

"I'm still upset that you left early." Frannie takes a sip of coffee from her *World's Greatest Sister* mug. It was a birthday gift from our older sister, Maya. I got one just like it, along with one of a matching pair of white T-shirts with the words '*Happy Birthday to Two*' printed across the chest in pink font. Frannie is wearing hers now. I stuffed mine into the bottom of my suitcase where I'll leave it for eternity. "Why do you need to talk to her? Does it have to do with the reason you ditched us?"

I didn't ditch. I took off because I'd felt completely out of place. Frannie married her high school sweetheart, Grant, before she finished college.

I was the odd woman out at our birthday dinner and my parents both made a point of mentioning it every chance they could.

There wasn't an extra bed at Frannie and Grant's place, so I ended up stuck on the sofa bed at my parents' condo. Waking up each morning to weak coffee and a discussion on how to find a husband gets old after five days.

It didn't help that *my* high school sweetheart and Grant's friend, Boyd, dropped by Frannie's house for a piece of birthday cake. My parents called it fate when they saw our hands touching. I called it an accident since it happened when I was handing him a slice of cake on a small dessert plate.

It's not like I'm going to live the rest of my life single and alone. I have a few decades left to find my soul mate. I wish my parents could see that.

Since they can't, I called the airline, switched my flight and left San Francisco with an excuse about needing to get back to my job as a vet assistant at Premier Pet Care.

Work is not part of my plan this week. I'm going to spend the rest of my time off pampering myself with bubble baths and window shopping.

"You're zoning out, Tilly." Frannie leans toward the screen of her tablet. "What's going on? You left in a rush and it's the middle of the morning there. If you needed to get back to work, why aren't you at the clinic?"

Dammit. I'm obviously still not thinking about anything other than Lisa's lover.

"I really need to talk to Maya. I was about to call her when you called me. "

The corners of her lips dip into a slight frown. I know she wants me to confide in her but I can't. If I tell Frannie that I saw a hot stranger without his pants on, half of San Francisco will know about it by noon.

She can't keep a secret and I don't need the added burden of having to explain to my dad what happened last night.

He's as old-fashioned as they come and in his world, a woman should be living at home until she's married.

Frannie did. Maya didn't. Instead, she moved across the country to New York City. I followed.

"Fine." She takes another sip of her coffee, waving the mug in front of the camera. "I am the world's greatest sister. I know you feel closer to Maya because you two live in the same city, but I love you as much as she does."

That tugs at my heart. "I love you too, Frannie. You know that I do."

"I know." She tilts her head to the left. "I'm here if you need me. You can tell me anything."

I can't.

How do I tell her that I when I woke up this morning I could hear the distinctive sound of a man's voice? I got out of bed, opened my bedroom door a crack and caught sight of the black-haired, blue-eyed, tattooed sex god from last night walking shirtless around my living room talking on a cell phone.

He was only wearing jeans. No shirt, no shoes, just sexiness for days.

I didn't say anything to him. I went back to bed and by the time I got up thirty minutes later he was nowhere to be seen.

I might have spent that half hour taking care of myself with my battery-operated boyfriend while thinking about Lisa's lover.

I shouldn't feel guilty about that, but I do.

"Tilly?" Frannie's voice breaks through my thoughts. "You're drifting away again."

I smile. "I'm jetlagged, Fran. I'll call you tonight. Have fun at the zoo today."

"Have fun doing whatever you ran back to New York to do." She leans closer to the screen before her voice falls to a whisper. "Or whoever you ran back to do."

Before I have a chance to say another word, she ends the video call by blowing me a kiss.

I immediately dial Maya's number but she doesn't pick up. I curse under my breath and call Julian, her fiancé. He's always told me to reach out if I can't get in touch with Maya, but it rings straight to his voicemail too.

I stifle a frustrated scream, race to my bathroom and jump into the shower so I can track down my older sister. I need to tell someone what I saw last night before I burst.

Chapter 3

Tilly

"Wait, what?" I stare at Maya's lips. "Say it slower this time, Maya. I think I heard you wrong. "

"I hope I heard you wrong. "Maya's fiancé, Julian Bishop, turns from where he's standing in the kitchen of their apartment. His hand runs through his black hair. "Maya, tell me that you didn't just say that you agreed to let Sebastian move into Tilly's place."

She shrugs. "I did, Julian."

"Why?" He stalks toward where we're standing near the doorway. "Maya, we talked about this repeatedly. I love you more than anything, but you can't change fate."

She kisses his cheek. "I have told you for months now that Tilly is perfect for Sebastian. This is my way of testing that theory. It benefits Tilly and Sebastian. She can cover rent and he has a place to live. For now, they're just roommates."

Her words float over me in a haze of confusion.

I'm still stuck back where she told me that the man I found in my apartment last night is Sebastian Wolf. I didn't get a chance to explain that I saw every inch of him before she blurted out that she agreed to let him move in with me.

She's been trying to set me up with the naked sex god for almost a year.

I've never been interested in him because he's a police officer. Technically, he's a homicide detective.

I've already dated three members of the NYPD and not one of those connections progressed past the second date. I had nothing in common with any of them.

Besides, he's Julian's best friend. I'm still getting to know Maya's future husband. I don't want to risk putting him in an awkward position. If I get involved with Sebastian and it ends badly, it could impact my relationship with Julian and my sister. I can't let that happen.

I always assumed I'd meet Sebastian in a suit at their wedding, not nude in my living room.

Maya owns my apartment. When she moved in with Julian, she gave me the go-ahead to do whatever I wanted to with the place. That included renting out the second bedroom.

Since I've lived there, I've always been the one to seek out roommates, I've vetted them and I've handled the signing of the rental agreements.

It was different with Lisa.

Maya is a real estate broker and Lisa happened to be one of her clients. She was going through a messy divorce when she and her soon-to-be ex-husband contracted Maya to sell their apartment.

Since I was looking for a roommate at the time, Maya called and asked if I'd be willing to live with Lisa.

I asked one question in response. "Can she pay half of the rent?"

When Maya assured me she could, I sent the rental agreement to Lisa's office. She signed and by the end of that week, she was moved in.

She committed to renting the extra bedroom for a year. She still has five months to go.

"What about Lisa?" I scratch the back of my head. "Is she sharing a room with him? It's a two bedroom, Maya. The master bedroom is mine and Lisa's bedroom is the other one, so where is he supposed to sleep?"

I suddenly wonder if he was camped out on the sofa all night in the nude.

"Lisa is in Tokyo." Maya lowers herself into the armchair next to us, adjusting the front of the soft gray dress she's wearing.

Both Julian and I turn at those words, but I ask the obvious question before he can even open his mouth. "Why is Lisa in Tokyo?"

"Family stuff." She slides a tube of lipstick out of her purse. "She said she had to take off and wouldn't be back for months. She wanted out of her lease agreement."

I watch as my older sister applies a pale shade of pink to her lips. Maya is beautiful. Her hair is black, her eyes the same shade of blue as mine. She's shorter than I am, but she carries herself with an elegant grace that has always turned heads, including her devoted fiancé who can't take his eyes off of her.

"Why didn't she call me about this?" I look down at the red sneakers I slipped my feet into when I left my apartment. I put on a chunky red sweater and a pair of black yoga pants before I hopped on the subway and raced over here. "I'm her roommate."

"You were on vacation. I didn't see the point in bothering you." She looks at the watch on her wrist. It doesn't work. My sister has never owned a watch that keeps time. She only wears them because she loves vintage timepieces. "Speaking of which, why are you back here? I thought you were hanging out in San Francisco for another few days. You got the gifts I sent to Frannie's place for your birthday, right?"

"I came back early because I missed you and I love the gifts," I lie, twice. "Don't change the subject, Maya. Why would you agree to let Sebastian move into my place without discussing it with me first?"

"He isn't officially your roommate until the end of the month." She scans the screen of her phone when it chimes. "I have a listing appointment in thirty minutes."

I nod. I've never gotten in the way of Maya's work. I've always understood when she's had to cancel dinner plans or movie dates with me to show a client a property or meet with another broker. This is the first time I've even been remotely tempted to ask her to postpone an appointment because of me, but I won't.

"Did you sell his apartment already, Maya?" Julian walks to where she's seated. He holds out a hand to help her stand.

Swoon. My future brother-in-law is the definition of a gentleman.

"Sebastian accepted an offer yesterday morning." She takes his hand and glides to her feet. "I meant to tell you last night, but we got…" she looks over at me. "Busy."

I roll my eyes, not wanting to hear about my sister's sex life, again.

"It's a fast close and the rental market is tight right now, so I told him he could stay with Tilly until he works something else out." She looks up at Julian. "I gave him the set of keys that Lisa dropped off at my office on her way to the airport. I mentioned that Tilly would be in California for a few more days, but he was more than welcome to go check out the apartment."

"I understand," he says because he's not the one who has to live with Sebastian Wolf.

"I don't." I put my hands on my hips. "Maya, you didn't even call me to ask if it would be all right with me."

"I was going to talk to you about it once you were back. I didn't realize he was planning on moving in as soon as I handed him the keys. I thought he'd hold off for at least a couple of weeks." She brushes past Julian. "Tilly, he's a good guy. He works long hours so you'll hardly see him."

"You're trying to run my life again," I whisper.

"No." She reaches to push my hair back behind my shoulders. "I'm trying to help one of Julian's friends. Give him a chance, sis. Can you do that?"

I look back at Julian. His blue eyes brighten as he smiles.

"I'll give it a chance," I agree softly. "I hope I don't regret it."

"You won't." She tugs me into a hug. "You're going to love Sebastian as much as Julian and I do."

Chapter 4

Sebastian

"This is why I live alone." My youngest brother, Liam, lets out a long exhale. "Maybe you're wrong and she didn't see your dick. "

"I'm not wrong," I reply as I look back at the closed door of his office. "You're sure I'm not interrupting you? There's a woman in the waiting room."

He skims his finger over the screen of the cell phone on his desk. "I've got five minutes before my next appointment."

You wouldn't know by looking at him that Liam is a grief counselor. He's wearing gray pants, a white button-down shirt and black shoes. That part fits the bill. It's the rest of him that doesn't.

His shirt sleeves are rolled up to reveal forearms covered in tattoos. His shoulder length dark blond hair is tied into a messy low knot and a beard covers his jaw.

Considering the fact that he towers above me a good two inches at six-foot-five, he's got an undeniable presence that can't be ignored.

"The woman who saw my dick last night is Julian's future sister-in-law." I pace in front of his desk. "She didn't come right out and say she saw me nude, but she could barely look at me."

"Maybe she's shy." He crosses his arms over his chest. "If she's not making a big deal about it, why are you?"

It's a valid question. I should have let it roll off me, but once I got back into my bedroom after Matilda went into hers, I let my imagination wander.

Julian is protective of Matilda because he's about to become part of her family. His fiancée, Maya, is even more vigilant when it comes to her younger sister. She told me to watch over Matilda, not flash her within the first ten seconds of seeing her.

I don't need this to come between one of my closest friends and myself. I have to address it before Julian hears about it from Matilda.

"Julian and I have been friends a long time. I don't want something like this to fuck it up."

"I hear you. Why are you living with this woman? Why not find another guy to live with?" Liam looks down at his phone again. "You've got two more minutes."

For most of the past ten years I've lived alone. It wasn't until a few months ago that I took on a roommate. It was a buddy from work who needed a place to hang his hat after his marriage went south.

He took over the second bedroom and then one night a week, his kids took over the apartment.

When he decided to get his own place, I saw it as the perfect time to make a change in my life.

I called Maya and set up a time to talk to her about the possibility of selling my apartment. I picked it up years ago at a reasonable price. I've kept an eye on the market so I knew that if I got out now, I'd pocket a nice profit.

She listed it and sold it within a week for the full asking price with a thirty-day close.

My salary as a homicide detective with the NYPD keeps a roof over my head, food on my table and clothes on my back, but the windfall from the sale of my current two-bedroom apartment is enough to set me up in a new place and pad my savings account at the same time.

"I didn't expect my place to sell that quickly," I say, walking toward his office door. "A decent priced rental is hard to come by right now. Maya said her sister had an extra spare room and the rent is low, so I grabbed it before someone else did."

"Why the rush to move in? You had some time before the new owner came knocking on your door, didn't you?" he asks.

"I had a couple of days off. It made sense to make the move while I had the time."

"It sounds like you made the right choice." Liam falls into step behind me.

"It's a good move for me right now." I turn and tap him in the middle of the chest with my knuckles. "I'll hang out there for a few months and then start looking for a new apartment to buy."

"Tell her you're sorry that you inadvertently showed her your dick." He puts his hand on the doorknob. "Don't make a big deal about it. Apologize and move on."

"You think?" I ask as he swings open the door.

"I know, " he responds with a pat on my back. "Now, get lost. I've got work to do."

***

"I'm Sebastian Wolf," I say, holding out my hand toward her as she closes the apartment door.

She looks down at my outstretched palm before her gaze slides to the table behind me. A smile tugs at the corners of her mouth. "I'm Matilda."

Matilda.

Maya calls her Tilly. Julian does too, but the first time he ever mentioned her to me he referred to her as Matilda.

I prefer it. It suits her.

She's beautiful. Her hair is long, brown and falling in waves around her shoulders. Her eyes are big and blue.

She can't be much taller than five-foot-six since I'm towering above her.

Her hand drops in mine for a quick shake before she tugs it away.

"Did you buy those?" She cants her head to the left. "There were some flowers in that vase that Maya and Julian bought for my birthday, but they're gone now."

I glance over my shoulder at the bouquet of mixed red and yellow blossoms I picked up at the florist down the street on my way home from Liam's office. "I noticed they were dead, so I thought I'd replace them with a new bunch."

She brushes past me to smell them. "They're beautiful."

No, she is.

I shake off the thought and weigh my next words. "Matilda, I need to say something."

She straightens. "What is it?"

I swallow, hoping that my instinct isn't steering me wrong. I want to clear the air so we can start off as roommates on the right foot. "I wasn't expecting you to come home last night."

"Maya told me that." She glances down briefly before her gaze locks on my face. "She said that she explained to you that I would be out of town for a few more days, but my plans changed. I had no idea who you were last night. I thought you were here to see my last roommate."

I don't see the point in prolonging this, so I dive in. "I don't know how long you were standing near the doorway when I noticed you, but if you saw me without..."

"I did," she admits as her gaze trails down my gray T-shirt and faded jeans. "I saw you by the window without any clothes on."

"I'm sorry." I scrub the back of my neck with my hand. "I don't want this to be a big deal."

"It's fine." She blows out a short breath. "We don't have to make it into a big deal."

"I would have had pants on if I knew you were on your way home."

"That's good to know," she says with a small smile. "Let's make a rule that if either of us is in a common area, we need to be dressed. Agreed?"

"Agreed." I shove my hands into the front pocket of my jeans. "I'll only take my clothes off in my bedroom or when I shower."

Her gaze goes to the flowers again before she looks directly at me. "Since we're in agreement that what happened last night isn't a big deal, I don't see any reason for either of us to mention it to Maya or Julian."

I had no intention of telling Julian that his future sister-in-law got a good look at my cock. "They won't hear about it from me."

"Good." She lets out an audible breath. "We can put it behind us now."

I can't tell if she's more relieved that we cleared the air or that I'm in agreement that what happened last night isn't any of Julian or Maya's business. Either way, I'm grateful that this conversation didn't end with me looking for a new place to live.

Chapter 5

Tilly

"Did you pass by a ridiculously hot man with black hair and blue eyes on your way up here?" I tug on the forearm of my best friend, Kate Wesley.

She steps into my apartment with a glance back over her shoulder. "No. Why?"

I take her purse and black trench coat from her before I hug her tightly. "It's a long story."

"I have time." She steps back to look at me, her hazel eyes scanning my face. "I left my assistant manager in charge. She'll handle the shop until I get back."

I know how hard it must have been for her to leave her boutique, Katie Rose Bridal, in the middle of the afternoon.

She practically lives there. It's where I met her six months ago when Maya invited me to go wedding dress shopping with her.

Maya didn't find a dress that day, but I found a new best friend.

Kate and I have been close ever since.

I almost called her last night when I saw Sebastian nude, but Kate had a date and since she rarely ventures out with any man, I didn't want to interrupt that or what could have been the morning after.

When I sent her a text message an hour ago asking about her date, she wrote back that it was a bust. That's when I told her that I was back in

Manhattan and had the surprise of my life when I got home.

She dropped everything to come over here to get the details face-to-face. Thankfully, Sebastian left just minutes before she arrived, otherwise I would have had to take Kate to the coffee shop down the block to get some privacy.

"Do you want some tea?" I start toward the kitchen.

"No, I'm good." She brushes her hand over the side seam of her red sheath dress chasing away a wayward thread. "Why are you back already? I thought you were hanging out in San Francisco for a few more days."

Kate was even more excited than I was when I booked my trip to the west coast. She's originally from California too, although she hasn't been back to the Golden State in years.

"I had enough family time. " I laugh. "I love my folks and Frannie, but it was twenty-four seven. I needed a break."

She nods softly. "I'm not going to complain that you cut your time with them short. I missed you like crazy."

Kate's boutique is only two blocks from where I work at Premier Pet Care. I take the short walk to see her during my lunch break at least a few times a week. If she's not overwrought with bridal consultations, we usually grab a sandwich to share and eat in the office at the back of her store.

"I missed you too." I squeeze her hand. "So your date last night wasn't Prince Charming?"

She tugs on the tip of her long blonde ponytail as she shakes her head from side-to-side. “I knew immediately that we weren’t a great fit, but I stayed through dinner and then took off.”

I motion toward the black leather sofa that Maya bought when she first furnished this place. Our tastes are similar, so I haven’t had to change anything since I moved in. “They can’t all be perfect, right?”

She laughs. “I’d settle for half-perfect. It’s been forever since I met a guy I clicked with.”

I can say the same. I haven’t found any man worth investing my heart in since I moved to Manhattan. That’s not for lack of trying. I’ve been on more blind dates than I can count. I’ve used three different dating apps to try and match up with a guy who is a good fit for me. I’ve had dinner with men I’ve met at work and I even went on a lunch date with one of the real estate brokers that Maya knows.

I dated two of those men for a couple of months, but neither relationship amounted to anything substantial.

She settles on the sofa, crossing her legs at the knee. “Why did you ask about a hot black-haired, blue-eyed man? Did you spend the night with someone?”

I sit next to her and laugh. “Technically, I guess I did.”

She looks at me. “What kind of an answer is that? Did you or did you not spend the night with a man?”

A series of short, hard raps at the apartment door startles us both.

"Dammit," I mutter under my breath as I push to my feet. "This is a doorman building. You'd think he could do his job."

One of the reasons I jumped at the chance to move into Maya's apartment when she moved out to live with Julian is because I viewed the doorman who stands watch in the lobby as extra security.

I had it all wrong.

All Junior, the doorman, does is stand around playing games on his phone while people march right past him on their way to the elevator. He must have missed the memo that explained that an integral part of his job is to phone the tenants to announce when a visitor has arrived.

I race across the room and swing the door open with a flourish.

"You're not Sebastian." A striking redheaded woman stares at me. "Who are you?"

"Who are you?" I counter because this is my apartment, which I think, affords me the right to ask the questions.

"I'm Wendy. Where's Sebastian?"

"Who is Sebastian?" Kate asks from behind me.

I turn back to look at her. "My new room…"

"The man who has my panties," Wendy interrupts as she pushes past me. "I want them back."

Chapter 6

Tilly

"Sebastian isn't here, " I say as I watch Wendy head directly toward where Kate is still sitting on the sofa with a confused look on her face. "Can't you just call him?"

"Who is Sebastian?" Kate repeats as she watches Wendy dig her hand behind one of the sofa's cushions.

"We sleep together sometimes," Wendy answers before I have a chance to say anything.

"Tilly?" Kate's brows pop up. "What's going on?"

I leave the apartment door ajar as I walk to where Kate is sitting. "Sebastian is Julian's friend. He's my new roommate."

"You have a new roommate?" Her gaze volleys from me to where Wendy is now on her hands and knees looking under the sofa.

It's obvious from this angle that Wendy still owns at least one pair of panties, thong panties to be precise. I look away not sure if I should tell her that her skirt has hiked up so far that we can both see her ass.

"You should leave." I direct that to Wendy even though I'm looking at the ceiling. "Sebastian isn't here so I think you should go."

"I bought those panties at Liore Lingerie." She gets back up to her feet. "They are worth too much for me to leave them as a souvenir."

"A souvenir?" I mutter under my breath. "Don't you think you should call Sebastian and talk to him about this?"

"Did you take them off here?" Kate stands and glances back at where she was just sitting. "I wasn't sitting on them, was I?"

I scrub both my hands over my face. All I wanted to do was tell my best friend that I saw my new roommate naked last night. Now, I realize that he wasn't wearing any clothes because he'd fucked this woman in my apartment before I got home.

Thank God traffic from LaGuardia was heavy or I could have walked in on Wendy taking it hard on my sofa.

"He took them off of me right here." Wendy points to the middle of the sofa. "He might have thrown them back over his head."

All three of us turn toward the center of the room.

"I don't see them," Kate offers. "What color are they?"

I try to catch her eye to give her a warning glance to stop encouraging Wendy.

"What color are what?" A masculine voice interrupts.

I don't have to look toward the door of my apartment to know who is standing there. The sound of that raspy, deep tone is unmistakable even though I've only had two brief conversations with him.

"Oh, wow," Kate whispers. "Tilly, is that him?"

"What are you doing here, Wendy?" he asks tightly.

"Sebastian." Wendy rounds the coffee table and heads straight for him. "There you are, baby. I came to get my panties back, but if you have time, I'll trade you the ones I have on now for the pair I was wearing last night."

Kate inches toward me as Sebastian looks in my direction.

"You have to get this pair off me first." Wendy plays with the bottom of her skirt. "They're red, lace, and totally see-through."

I can attest to that.

"That's your new roommate?" Kate asks softly as she nudges her elbow into my side. "That's the surprise that was waiting for you last night?"

"That's him," I answer in a whisper. "He was here when I got home."

I look back at Sebastian and Wendy. He has yet to respond to her offer about her panties. I'm grateful. I already know too much about what the two of them did in my apartment last night.

"I shoved them in your purse when you were leaving," he finally says. "You should have called me before coming over here."

Wendy walks over to where she dropped her oversized red leather tote bag on the floor when she first arrived. She picks it up and fishes her hand in it before she tugs out a handful of black lace. "Well, shit. I guess I should have checked here first."

Sebastian stalks back toward the door. "I'll see you to the elevator, Wendy."

"You want me to go?" Her gaze glides over Kate and me. "Who are they?"

He turns back to look at us. "That's Matilda, my roommate, and…"

"I'm Kate." She rushes across the room with her hand outstretched. "I'm Tilly's best friend."

Sebastian reaches to shake her hand. "I'm Sebastian Wolf. It's a pleasure to meet you."

"The pleasure is all mine." Kate smiles up at him before she turns to me and winks. "I think Tilly is going to love having you for a roommate."

Chapter 7

Sebastian

I stand outside the door of the apartment after walking Wendy to the elevator.

She tried her best to convince me to go back to her place for a repeat of last night, but I declined.

We hook up every few months when there's no one else in the picture for either of us.

It's easy, fun and there are no strings attached. We meet up, fuck and go our separate ways until the urge strikes again.

It was Wendy who reached out yesterday and since I had my new place all to myself, and a scheduled day off today, I invited her over for a beer.

She left a couple of hours after she arrived with a satisfied grin on her face that mirrored my own.

Seeing her standing next to Matilda earlier was jarring. I could see Matilda putting the pieces together in her head. She knew I fucked Wendy in our apartment. It shouldn't matter since we're just roommates but it irritated the hell out of me that Wendy showed up without calling me first.

Before I have a chance to reach for the doorknob, the apartment door swings open.

"Sebastian," Kate says my name as she looks at me. "I was just leaving."

"You don't have to go." I move to the side to allow her to pass. "I can take off for a couple of hours and give you two some privacy."

She waves the smartphone that's clutched in her palm in the air. "There's an emergency at my shop. I need to get back there now."

Emergency.

The word is overused, but it still piques my interest. "What's the emergency?"

"He's a police detective." Matilda steps into the doorway and shoots me a teasing glance. "I think it's a requirement of his job to ask about emergencies."

I bow my head briefly to hide a smile.

Kate nods at her before she turns her attention back to me. "I own a bridal store. Today's emergency is a too-tight dress for a ceremony the day after tomorrow."

"That sounds serious." My mouth quirks.

"I had to call for back up." She giggles at her joke. "My seamstress is already on the case, but I need to go calm down the bride-to-be."

"Do you want to meet up for dinner later?" Matilda brushes her hand over Kate's shoulder. "I can come by the shop with some take-out."

Kate shakes her head. "I'm taking you out to celebrate your birthday. Put on that cute little black dress you bought last month and meet me at the shop at eight. We can grab an Uber from there."

A wide smile slides over Matilda's lips.

Jesus, she's breathtaking.

"I'll be there." She brushes past me to walk her friend to the elevator.

"It was good meeting you," Kate calls back to me as I step inside the apartment. "I'm sure I'll see you again."

She will. I'm already enjoying this new living arrangement.

***

I exhale harshly, trying to absorb what Matilda just said to me.

She repeats the words as she closes the door to the apartment behind her. "I said that I think you should move out."

"Why?" I rake my hand through my hair. I know the answer to that question, but I ask it anyway.

"I've never lived with a man before," she begins before she turns to look at the vase full of flowers. "Wendy said that you two had fun last night and that's great. I'm all for having fun."

I move so I'm standing directly in front of her. "What's the problem, Matilda?"

Her eyes skim my T-shirt before they land on my face. "I wouldn't call it a problem."

"What would you call it?" I cross my arms over my chest and her gaze immediately drops to my biceps.

"I don't think we're compatible."

What the fuck does that mean? We've lived together for less than a day.

I've learned that beating around the bush is a waste of time so I dive right into the crux of the matter. "You were surprised when Wendy showed up."

She dips her chin. "Yes. I didn't expect that."

"I didn't either," I confess softly. "We don't see each other often. I thought when she left last night that I wouldn't see her again for months."

That draws her gaze to mine. "So it's a casual thing?"

"Very casual. Very infrequent."

She fights back a smile. "I thought she was your girlfriend."

I rub my jaw. "I don't have a girlfriend. I don't have room in my life for my job and a relationship so you don't have to worry about a woman hanging out here with me all the time."

She pinches the bridge of her nose. "My last roommate and I had an understanding. If she had a guy over, she'd close her bedroom door. I did the same."

Why the fuck is my stomach knotting hearing her talking about having a guy in her bedroom?

"That worked out for us, but I think if you keep living here, we need to take it a step further. What about a heads-up text if one of us is planning on having company?"

Her voice wavers with the last word, but I can tell she's got more to say so I don't interrupt.

"I'm not suggesting that you can't be here if I have a man with me," she goes on. "I'm just saying that the respectful thing to do is to let each other know if we're not coming home alone or if we invite someone over."

"Understood." My jaw tightens. "I'll keep that in mind the next time I have a guest."

Her hands go to her hips. "Today made me uncomfortable, Sebastian. Wendy said you took off her panties on the sofa and I saw you nude when I got home, so I know you two…well, I know stuff happened on my sofa."

Stuff? I slid Wendy's panties off before she took off in the direction of Matilda's room with a bare ass. I had to chase her down to steer her toward my bedroom.

"Nothing happened there." I motion toward the sofa with my hand.

She glances back before her eyes lock on mine. "Maya told me that you owned an apartment before you moved in here, so I'm sure you did whatever you wanted wherever you wanted."

I scratch my chin. "I'm not going to do anything that makes you uncomfortable. You set the rules and I'll follow them."

"It might be easier for you to find another place to live."

"I sold my place furnished and I've already moved the rest of my things in." I point at my bedroom door. "I'll be at work more than I'll be here and I'll never be late with my half of the rent."

"Will you text me a warning and keep your bedroom door closed when Wendy comes over?" She arches a brow. "Or any of your other friends?"

The way she enunciates the word *friends* is adorable.

If I thought she was interested in me at all, I might mistake her reaction to Wendy's impromptu visit as jealousy.

"Maya gave me your number so I'll text a warning and I'll keep my door closed."

"You can stay for now." She tilts her head. "The rules are simple, Sebastian. I'll stay out of your way if you stay out of mine."

"You won't even know I'm here."

That lures a smile to her lips. "You won't know I'm here either."

With that she turns and walks away, the sway of her perfectly round ass taunting me with every step she takes.

Chapter 8

Tilly

"The last time I met a man as handsome as Sebastian, was the day I met…" Kate's voice trails as she realizes what she was about to say.

We both know the name that almost left her lips.

Gage. Gage Burke.

He's the man who broke her heart. He took off right before their wedding, leaving her to face three hundred guests and the rest of her life alone.

That was back in California. It's been years and she's dating other men now, but Gage owns a piece of her heart that I don't think she'll ever get back.

I've never met him, but a part of me loathes him for hurting her.

"Sebastian is good looking." I shrug as I drag my fork through a small pile of spring peas on my plate. "That doesn't mean I'm completely okay with him being my roommate."

"Good looking?" she echoes with a smile. "He's the kind of hot that makes a woman forget her own name. I saw the way he was looking at you."

I take a bite of the salmon I ordered, weighing whether I should even ask what she means by that.

"He couldn't take his eyes off of you, " she goes on without any prompting from me. "He likes you."

"He doesn't like me," I protest. "I'm the sister of his best friend's fiancée."

"What does that have to do with anything?"

"He has to be nice to me because of Julian and Maya." I dab at my mouth with the linen napkin. "Maya agreed to let him move in without talking to me about it. Lisa left town, he took over the second bedroom and I was completely out of the loop even though it's my place."

Technically, I know it's my sister's apartment, but it still stings that I left town a few days ago only to return to find a new roommate.

"So, you came home early and found him there?" She cuts a slice of her duck breast. "It must have scared the hell out of you."

"Actually," I begin before I take a sip of red wine. "He wasn't wearing any clothes when I walked in."

Her fork drops to her plate. "What? He was naked?"

"Naked." I confirm with a smile as I set my glass down. "He was standing by the window in the living room. He had earbuds in so he didn't notice me right away."

Her hand leaps to my wrist. "What exactly did you see?"

"Everything," I say in a low tone. "I saw everything."

"His cock?" she shoots back quickly, her voice an octave higher than it was seconds ago. "You saw his cock?"

I steal a brief glance at the couple seated at the table next to us, but they're so lost in each other's eyes, they don't even flinch at Kate's words.

I never imagined that the first time I'd have dinner at Nova that the conversation would be centered on a penis. I doubt anyone else in this Michelin-starred restaurant is having a discussion similar to ours.

"I saw it," I answer with a nod.

She leans back in her chair, her hands falling to her lap. "He's big, isn't he? Wendy was practically drooling all over herself when he walked in. It was obvious that she wanted more of what she got last night."

I run my hand over my forehead. "We're not actually having this discussion, are we?"

"What?" She laughs. "You just told me that you saw your roommate naked. Naturally, I want to know if he's bigger than average."

"He is," I whisper although I don't know what's considered average. All I know for sure is that Sebastian is well endowed.

"What did he say when he realized you were staring at his cock?" Kate downs a sip of wine.

I run my fingertip over the edge of my plate. "He didn't say anything last night, but he did bring it up earlier. He said he didn't want to make a big deal out of it."

Her gaze skims my face. "Do you think it's a big deal?"

I shrug. "He thought I was in California. He fucked Wendy, she left and I showed up. It was awkward, but it doesn't have to be a big deal."

She tilts her head. “You’re living with a hot-as-sin man that you’ve seen naked. I’d say that’s a big deal.”

I laugh. “Last night was the one and only time I’ll ever see Sebastian Wolf naked. He works crazy long hours. I doubt I’ll see much of him at all anymore.”

She lifts her wine glass in the air. “In that case, let’s toast to last night and your photographic memory.”

“Who says I have a photographic memory?” I pick up my glass.

“A woman always remembers the sight of a magnificent cock.” She touches her glass against mine. “Cheers to that.”

Chapter 9

Sebastian

"What the fuck do you think you're doing?" I slam the door behind me, but not before my words reach the man sitting at the desk I just barged past. I see him stand out of the corner of my eye but he knows better than to race in here to get between his boss and me.

"Detective Wolf." My asshole of a friend, Darrell Carver, gives me a look from where he's standing next to a row of bookcases. "To what do I owe the pleasure of this visit?"

"Go to hell." I lower myself into a chair in front of his desk. I don't give a fuck that my back is to him or that he happens to be an assistant district attorney. "I heard that you're cutting Justin Beacon loose. Tell me my lieutenant is mistaken."

"As usual, your lieutenant has the facts straight. That woman is never wrong." He walks past me to the worn leather office chair behind his desk.

It's been there since I became a detective four years ago. Darrell is the third person that I've seen in the chair. The rigors of the job were too much for his last two predecessors.

So far, he's holding his own but he's yet to mark his seventh month on the job. There's a running bet in my squad room about how long he'll make it. My money is on a couple of weeks shy of a year.

The strands of gray hair at his temples speak to the stress he's under. The tan lines where his wedding ring once sat on his left hand only add to the story of how drastically his life has changed since he accepted this position.

"I gave you everything you needed to put him away for life." I scrub my hand over the back of my neck, irritation gnawing at me. "Now, you're about to let a fucking murderer walk free."

"Sebastian." His voice takes on the calm tone that I loathe when we're anywhere but grabbing a beer at my favorite pub. Our relationship has two distinct facets.

After hours we're friends.

As a detective and assistant district attorney we rarely see eye-to-eye.

I work hard to find justice for people who have lost their lives at the hands of another. I do what it takes to drop them at Darrell's feet with as much ammunition as I can to put them away forever.

"One of our witnesses died. The other flipped his story on its end." He exhales. "I don't have a case without them."

It's been months since I arrested Beacon for the murder of a friend of his. The nineteen-year-old almost cracked in the interrogation room under my questioning before my lieutenant pulled me out.

It was for the same reason it always is. The sight of Beacon's friend's lifeless body fueled my temper. He'd bled out from a stab wound to the chest.

I didn't touch the fucking asshole, but my fists made contact with the wooden table in the interrogation room one too many times according to Christine Hildebrandt, my lieutenant.

Once Beacon asked for a lawyer, I set out to find as much evidence as I could while he sat in a cell unable to make bail. Now, six months later, the son-of-a-bitch is set to walk free.

"You can't work with what you have left?" I shove a hand through my hair. "What about the blood on the sole of his shoe?"

"He's the one who called 9-1-1." Darrell shakes his head. "He had as much blood on his shoes as the paramedics. I won't win this. Without those witnesses, we've got nothing."

"I'll talk to the surviving witness," I offer. "Give me ten minutes with him."

"That's not happening." He leans back in his chair. "He left the country a month ago. It's over, Sebastian. As much as I wish we could, we can't win every case."

"We should," I bark back. "How did Leonard's mother take the news that her son's killer isn't going to pay for what he did?"

His eyes meet mine. I see the answer before he says a word. "Just as you'd expect."

I'd expect the woman to fall apart. Leonard Grilson's mom, Betty, had one child.

I'll never forget the look on her face when I went to her apartment to tell her he had died. The pain in her voice was palpable. Just as it is every single fucking time I have to walk into someone's home to tell them their life will never be the same again because a person they love was killed.

I promised Betty her son's death wouldn't be in vain.

Now, I'm a fucking liar and she has to live the rest of her days knowing that her kid's childhood friend shoved a knife through his heart because of an unpaid loan of a few hundred dollars.

"That's on us." I stand and button my suit jacket. "Her pain is on us."

"No." Darrell rises to his feet. "It's on Justin Beacon."

I rest my palms on the top of his desk as I lean forward. "It was our job to put that bastard away, Darrell."

He raises both hands in the air. "I did my best."

"It's not good enough." I cock a brow in challenge.

His arms cross over his chest. "Get on this side, Sebastian. Go to law school, sit in this chair and do your best. I guarantee you won't do a better job than I am."

"Fuck you." I straighten my stance. "I'd do better. We both know I would."

"Prove it." He smiles. "You'd make a great lawyer. You should have stuck with your first instinct."

I laugh as I turn to leave. "Beers next Tuesday night at Easton Pub, Darrell. You're buying."

"Sure," he calls as I open the door to his office. "I'm not joking about law school. Go. It's what you're meant to do."

Darrell is one of only a handful of people who knows that I was accepted into law school years ago.

I didn't pursue it. Instead I followed in my father's footsteps by joining the force. Turning my life upside down to become a lawyer isn’t going to happen. I left that dream in my past.

Chapter 10

Tilly

"I thought you were asleep, Matilda."

I glance over to where Sebastian is standing in the hallway. He's only wearing a pair of black pajama pants.

I heard him come in less than an hour ago. It was just past midnight. I was in my room watching a video on my laptop that Frannie sent me of her latest obsession.

Apparently, my twin was serious when she told me last week that she was going to start sewing matching dresses for her daughters. They are a year-and-a-half apart, but Fran has such fond memories of the two of us being dressed alike when we were kids, that she wants to "*recreate that magic*" with her girls.

I couldn't help but laugh when she called it magic.

I hated being forced to dress just like my twin until we graduated from middle school. Most of our close friends could tell us apart since Frannie chipped one of her bottom teeth when she fell off her bike when we were seven-years-old.

Everyone else in our school called me Frannie first before I corrected them. It made sense to them given the fact that she was more popular than I was.

"I could say the same." I tighten the sash of my short blue silk robe. "I'm just grabbing a glass of juice."

"Pour one for me too." He motions to the cupboard that holds the glasses. "I dropped some money on the counter for food before I left for work. I want to pay for half of every expense."

I nod. I was surprised when I woke up early this morning and found two hundred dollars on the counter next to a handwritten note from him. He wrote down his cell number alongside an explanation that I should use the number if I ever need to text or call him. He also wrote that he ate a bowl of my favorite cereal and wanted to pay for half of our combined food costs for the month.

"I've never spent more than a hundred dollars a month on groceries." I reach into the cupboard and grab a small glass. "I put most of your money in the top drawer of the foyer table. Fifty a month is good."

He approaches and reaches for the glass of orange juice after I fill it. "One hundred a month for food? It all makes sense now."

I lean my hip against the counter, tugging the top of my robe together with one hand. It was the only thing I put on after I had a bath. "What makes sense?"

"The fact that you have no food in your refrigerator other than this juice, a carton of milk and what looks like an apple with something growing on it. Maybe it isn't an apple. It could be a tomato, or was a tomato."

I take a drink to ward off a smile. "I get take-out most nights."

"I did too when I was your age." He arches a dark brow.

I try to keep my eyes trained to his face, but the man has a six-pack and a trail of dark hair that dips below the waistband of his pajama pants. Even though I've already seen what's hidden under the fabric, I sense the uptick in my heart rate just from thinking about what his cock looks like. I also feel my nipples harden.

Maybe Kate was right about that photographic memory thing.

I shake off the thought. "When you were my age? You're not that much older than I am."

"I'm thirty-two."

I know that. Maya told me a lot about him when she was trying to get me to agree to have dinner with him. He went to high school with Julian. I did the math.

"I'm twenty-five," I offer although I have a feeling that's not a surprise to him.

"I know," he confirms with a nod of his head. "When I was twenty-five I survived on burgers and fries."

"I prefer salads." I lie with a smile. I don't think Sebastian cares what I eat, but for some inexplicable reason, I want him to see me as someone other than a woman who chows down on greasy burgers and dozens of fries whenever a craving strikes.

I'm taking full advantage of my rapid metabolism while I can.

"Don't get me wrong." He takes another sip from his glass. "I still eat junk food more than I should, but I supplement with fruits and vegetables."

His large hand falls to his rock hard stomach. "I made a vow to myself that I'd stay in shape for at least another decade or two."

My gaze follows the motion of his hand. Every move he makes is mesmerizing. I should remind him of our rule about being fully dressed when in a common area, but I'd rather stare in silence at his muscular arms and chest.

"I can't promise I'll be around most nights, but we can split the cooking duties if you want."

"No," I say, laughing. "I can't."

"You can't?" he asks, setting his empty glass in the sink. "Or you won't? If you don't cook because you hate the cleanup, I'll load the dishwasher."

I look down at the front of the stainless steel dishwasher. "I don't know if it works. I've never used it."

He scratches his jaw as his eyes scan my face. "You wash dishes by hand?"

I sigh. "I wash my glass or mug by hand. It's not like I have enough dishes for a load. Lisa never ate here, so she didn't use it."

"Do you ever cook?"

"I made Maya macaroni and cheese once when she was living here." I smooth my tongue over my bottom lip. "She handled the dishes that day."

His mouth twitches. "I'll cook for you, Matilda. When our schedules sync and we're both home around dinner time, I'll make something for the two of us."

"You don't have to do that." I inch back, suddenly feeling a wave of heat rush over me. "I'm happy with take-out."

"I'll cook you dinner," he insists as he leans closer to me. "Consider it a thank you for letting me rent the extra room."

I should clarify that I had zero say in that, but I don't. "It's late. We should head to bed."

His full lips curve into a sly grin.

Shit. I didn't mean it like that.

I glance down and my eyes zero in on the front of his pajama pants and the obvious outline of his now semi-hard cock.

My gaze shoots up again to his face. "I meant that I should go to my room and you'll go to the other bedroom."

He runs a hand through his now messy hair. "I'm going to sit up for a bit, but I hope you sleep well."

There's a part of me that wants to sit with him, even if it's just to stare at his profile while he gets lost in his thoughts. He's doing that now. His jaw is clenching and his fist is tightening around the edge of the counter.

"Sebastian," I say his name softly.

He raises a brow in silent response.

"I hope when you do go back to bed, that you sleep well too."

The corners of his mouth rise in a gentle smile. "I haven't slept well in years. Insomnia comes with the job."

I nod, even though I have a million questions begging to be asked. He's just my roommate. We barely know each other and when he doesn't offer any more details about why sleep eludes him; I turn and walk back to my bedroom, closing the door behind me.

Chapter 11

Sebastian

I wanted to follow Matilda into her room last night.

I haven't felt a woman's arms wrapped around me in pure comfort in years.

The way she was looking at me made me feel like I'd be safe in her bed, in her embrace, pressed next to her body as I drifted off to sleep.

When she closed the door to her bedroom I settled on the sofa, my gaze pinned to the window and the lights of the city beyond.

I sat there for hours thinking. I finally dragged my ass back to my bedroom at three. I slept until my alarm woke me at six-thirty.

I was showered, dressed in a gray suit and white shirt and on my way to work by seven.

"You look like shit, partner."

I don't look up from my desk. I know that voice all too well. Samuel Brant is standing next to me.

He landed in homicide five months ago with that wide-eyed look and frenetic energy all new detectives share.

It's slowly wearing away now, replaced with the jaded view of New York City that every person in this squad room now has.

"I'm tired," I reply with a forced laugh. "I was here a hell of a lot later than you were last night."

"I have a girlfriend, " he points out with a tap of his fingers on the edge of my desk. "I need to kiss her goodnight in my own special way every night."

I finally look up at him. He's younger than me by three years. His brown hair is cut short. His blue eyes are a shade lighter than mine. I've got a few inches on him, and I outweigh him by a solid twenty pounds, but he holds his own.

He sprinted past me last week during a foot chase of a suspect. He wrestled the guy to the ground with ease. I was impressed and told him as much.

"I don't need the details, Brant." I shake my head. "I also don't need a girlfriend. I get the opportunity to kiss women good night in my special way whenever the mood strikes."

"Have you ever been married?" He takes a seat behind his desk. It faces mine. Our lieutenant is convinced that it encourages better communication between partners. I'm convinced that it breeds hostility.

I've never found a perfect rhythm with a partner. Samuel is my fifth since I was assigned to this division. There's a reason I'm nicknamed *Lone Wolf* in the squad room.

No one has ever said it to my face, but I hear the whispered insults behind my back. I don't always follow procedure to a tee. I do what's needed to close the cases I'm assigned, within the blurred boundaries of the law, of course.

"No." I shake my head. "You?"

"I'm considering it." He looks down at his left hand. "My girl is the one. I'm running out of reasons not to pop the question."

The job should be reason enough.

Most of the detectives in homicide are married to it. Those that have someone at home waiting for them are the lucky ones. They found a lover willing to put up with the long hours, moderate pay and emotional demons that haunt every one of us.

I stopped looking for a woman who would tolerate this bullshit years ago.

"What's her name?" I ask because he looks like a kid who just raided a candy store. The smile on his face is a testament to how much he loves his girlfriend.

"Remy."

"I'd say Remy could do better." I lean my forearms on my desk. "But she could do worse too."

He huffs out a laugh. "I'm the best man for her. She knows it."

I turn my attention back to my computer screen. If she loves him as much as he loves her, they'll stand a chance. That's if he doesn't let the job become his mistress. Once that happens his happily-ever-after will be out of his reach.

***

"What the hell, Donald?" I stare in disbelief at the asshole sitting on the sofa in my living room.

Matilda's living room? Our living room? It doesn't fucking matter.

Donald Crimpton jerks to his feet. "Detective Wolf? How? Why?"

"Sebastian?" Matilda's voice comes at me from the left.

I instinctively stalk toward her, blocking her body from Donald's view.

It's a smart move considering the fact that she's wearing a killer red dress and matching heels.

The neckline of the dress is low enough to give both Donald and me a perfect view of the top of her tits.

I swear to fuck I'm in the middle of a nightmare right now, but I'm wide-awake. It's just past seven o'clock, and I'm finally home after a long day filled with paperwork and false leads.

"What's going on?" Matilda asks. "Do you two know each other?"

I look down at her. "Do you two know each other?"

She nods. "We're about to go on our second date."

"You're not going anywhere with him," I say gruffly.

Her blue eyes widen as her hands fall to her hips. "Excuse me? What's the problem, Sebastian?"

"I answered all your questions two months ago, Detective Wolf." Donald squeaks from somewhere behind me. "How did you know I'd be here? Is Tilly working undercover or something? Is she wearing a wire? I'm pretty sure my lawyer would say that's entrapment."

I fist my hands at my side, not bothering to turn around to face him. "I live here, asshole."

"You're kidding." He snorts out a nervous laugh. "Since when?"

"He moved in a few days ago." Matilda tries to move around me but I take a step to the side to block her. "What's going on?"

"You moved in here because of my case?" The piece-of-trash asks. "I didn't see anything, Detective Wolf. You're wasting your time if you think I'm going to confess to witnessing an attempted murder."

"A what?" Matilda grabs hold of my forearm. "What the hell is he talking about?"

I exhale harshly, pissed that she's been dragged into the shittiest part of my life.

"I was at a party where a guy got hit over the head." Donald moves to stand next to me. "Detective Wolf is convinced I saw something. I didn't."

He did. I know full well he did because there's cell phone footage of him leaving the bedroom where the assault occurred after the 9-1-1 call was made. The caller, who was at the party, reported hearing a fight.

I was dragged out of bed by a call from my lieutenant to check out the situation.

The doctor working in the emergency room didn't think the victim would make it, but he's on the road to a full recovery.

The perpetrator was covered in blood. I finally got him to confess. He's already worked out a plea deal so Donald's useless to me at this point.

"The case is closed." I turn to look at Donald. He's a twenty-two-year-old troll who lives high on his folks' money. "You'd think your buddy would have clued you into that by now."

"I didn't know anyone at that party." He sticks to the same song-and-dance that first poured out of his lying mouth the night of the attack.

"Your cell phone records prove otherwise." I seethe. "You're not welcome here."

"That's for Tilly to decide, isn't it?" He looks at her with obvious lust.

I want to jab a finger in each of his eye sockets.

"Leave now, Donald." She steps closer to me, pointing at the door. "Our first date was our last date."

"Your loss," he quips. "I would have shown you the time of your life tonight."

Her gaze meets mine as he leaves our apartment, slamming the door behind him.

Chapter 12

Tilly

I need to stop with the dating apps. What the hell is wrong with me? I was about to have dinner, and then most likely sleep with a man who was involved in an attempted murder case.

I don't care if he was a witness, an accomplice or if he was the person who did it.

The way Sebastian reacted to him was enough to make me want to cut Donald out of my life for good.

I can't say I'm disappointed.

The only reason I agreed to a second date was that the kiss at the end of our first date held promise.

I almost let my libido guide me into bed with another jerk.

"I should probably run the name of every guy I'm about to go on a date with past you first," I joke as I look at Sebastian's face.

My attempt at humor to break the silence doesn't work.

He's still scowling. He hasn't moved an inch even though Donald stormed out of the apartment at least three minutes ago.

"Where did you meet him?" he questions.

I'd bet my last dollar that Sebastian doesn't have any dating apps on his phone. The man could walk out of our building without a shirt on, and he'd have a handful of potential fuck partners within seconds.

"On a dating app," I confess. "We have a lot in common."

"Like what?" His chin lifts.

Seriously? Do I need to answer that?

His silent stare tells me I do.

"He likes animals and since I'm a vet assistant, that matched up." I stop and take a breath. "He's a fan of Broadway musicals. You wouldn't know that from looking at him, but he told me that he could score tickets to that new show that everyone is raving about."

His gaze narrows. "You need to stay away from guys like that."

This conversation feels like it's slipping closer to lecture territory, so I attempt to stop it in its tracks. "Another rule that Lisa and I had was that we didn't talk about who we were dating or sleeping with."

"You slept with him?" He takes a step closer to me. "When he said he would have shown you the time of your life I assumed he meant a first fuck, but that happened already?"

I look down at my dress. My breasts are heaving and that's not because I'm trying to look sexy. I'm breathing heavily. It's a combination of the adrenaline rush of finding out that Donald wasn't who I thought he was and hearing Sebastian talk about fucking.

"We didn't." I shake my head. "It was just a kiss."

"A kiss?" His brows jump in surprise. "You kissed him?"

I run my hand along the side of my neck, feeling flush. "It was more of a peck after our first date last month. A goodnight, so-long-until-next-time kiss."

That lures a smile to his mouth. "Good to know."

I look back toward my closed bedroom door. "I'm going to change my clothes and then make some microwave popcorn for dinner."

"Don't change." His eyes meet mine as I turn back when he speaks. "We're going for spaghetti."

"Spaghetti," I echo. "We're going out for dinner?"

"You're all dressed up." He rakes me from head to toe. "You haven't eaten yet. I haven't either. Let's go grab some pasta."

My pulse thrums at the thought of spending an evening with him. My heart shouldn't be racing. He's not suggesting a date.

We're just two people going out to share a meal.

"After you, Matilda." He motions toward the apartment door. "You're about to have the experience of a lifetime."

"I am?" I ask with a smile. "How so?"

He rests his hand against the small of my back. "Come with me and I'll show you."

***

Sebastian wasn't joking. This is an experience I'm never going to forget.

I've had a lot of spaghetti in my life but none as delicious as this.

The pasta at Calvetti's is in a class of its own. It's handmade with a rich sauce and spicy meatballs. I've almost eaten every bite of food on my plate.

Sebastian finished his ten minutes ago.

"I told you it was amazing." He smiles broadly. "I can't believe you've never been here."

"I can't either." I laugh. "Maya's been here with Julian. It was on one of their first dates."

I leave out the extra X-rated information my sister provided about Julian touching her under the table while they were sitting in one of the booths that line the back wall. My gaze darts in that direction to a couple seated next to each other, kissing with fervor.

Maybe that's part of Calvetti's experience.

You come for the pasta and stay to come.

I shake off my ill attempt at a new slogan for this quaint family run restaurant.

"Do you use dating apps to meet men often?" he asks in a low tone.

I swallow a sip of red wine. "I wouldn't say it's often, but I've met a few great guys that way."

"Great?" He eyes me suspiciously as he reaches for the glass of ice water in front of him. It's the only thing he's drinking tonight. "Yet you're still looking."

I sigh heavily. "Isn't part of the fun the search?"

"The search for the one?" He draws out the last word.

"Until tonight I would have answered yes to that question." I laugh softly. "My sisters both found their Prince Charming. I was looking for mine too."

"You're not anymore?" His brow furrows.

I lock eyes with him. He's a beautiful man. His jaw is covered with late day scruff that only adds to his allure. His inky hair is thick and the perfect length for a woman's fingers to get lost in. His features are strong and his shoulders broad.

If someone had asked me six months ago to draw a picture in my mind's eyes of what my ideal man would look like, it would be Sebastian right down to the small mole on the right side of his neck under his ear.

There's nothing about him I'd change.

"I'm looking for someone who thinks that the best place in the world is next to me." I gaze down at my glass of wine. "I'm not sure I'll find him, but I know that after tonight, I'm deleting every dating app I have on my phone."

The moment is broken when the owner of the restaurant approaches us with a large piece of tiramisu on a plate with two forks.

Sebastian smile brightens as the older woman sets the plate down between us. "You're the best, Martina."

Her gaze darts from my face to his. She says something in Italian to him and he nods sagely.

Once she's out of earshot, I pick up one of the forks. "What did she say?"

He hesitates briefly before he dives his fork into the corner of the dessert. "She said you're beautiful."

I cast my gaze down to hide my wide smile.

"She's right," he says quietly as the jarring ring of a cell phone interrupts us.

I glance at my purse out of instinct, but his phone is in his hand before I have a chance to fish mine out.

"Sebastian Wolf," he answers succinctly as his eyes meet mine. "I'll be there in twenty minutes. Call Brant. He's closer. He'll take the lead on this one."

"You need to go to work," I state the obvious when he ends the call. "I'll get home on my own."

"I can take you." He stands and buttons his gray suit jacket.

"I'd like to stay." I eye the dessert. "I'll have another couple of bites of this and then I'll grab an Uber."

"Promise me you won't take the subway dressed like that." A grin ghosts his mouth.

"I promise."

"I'll get the check on my way out." He glances toward the door before his gaze falls back on me.

"Thank you for dinner. " I fumble in my mind with what to say next but he jumps in before I have a chance to get in another word.

"I'll likely be out all night so lock up tight and sleep well."

With that he's headed toward Martina and I'm left with a desperate need to know more about my new roommate.

Chapter 13

Tilly

"What's with all the food?" Kate says as she looks in my refrigerator for a bottle of water. "I take it Sebastian went grocery shopping?"

I wrinkle my nose at her. "I did."

"You?" She unscrews the cap of a bottle of sparkling lemon water. "Tilly Baker set foot in a grocery store and came out with more than a pre-made sandwich? What's this world coming to?"

I try to keep a straight face. "You're not funny."

"I've known you for how long?" She approaches where I'm already curled up on the sofa. "Six months or so and I've never seen your refrigerator that packed."

"Sebastian told me he likes fruits and vegetables." I shrug.

She sits next to me, brushing my feet to the side. "So because you're such a stellar roommate, you went to get him an assortment of his favorite foods?"

I don't take my eyes from the television screen because I know she's got a wide grin on her face. "It wouldn't hurt me to eat healthier, Kate."

"You're crushing on your new roomie."

I laugh. "No. I used the food money he gave me to buy groceries. It's as simple as that."

"It has nothing to do with the fact that he's well-hung and gorgeous?"

I shift so I'm facing her directly. "It's the middle of the afternoon on a Saturday. Why aren't you at work?"

A smile blooms on her lips. "I needed an afternoon off and since I don't have a roommate, I thought I'd come over here and hear about the adventures of your naked one."

I shoot her a look. "I saw him naked once. Every other time I've seen him, he's been dressed."

"That's disappointing." She adjusts the belt of her black dress. "I take that to mean that he hasn't visited your bedroom yet."

"Yet?" I slide to my feet and picked up my empty plate from the coffee table. I'd cut up an apple and an orange and had eaten my makeshift fruit salad after I got back from my mid-morning outing.

After I woke, I'd showered and dressed in jeans and a white sweater with the intention of going to my favorite diner, Crispy Biscuit, for brunch. On my way there I passed a storefront with a vibrant display of fruit. I picked up a few things and came back here to relax with a cup of coffee, hoping Sebastian would be awake.

It wasn't until I glanced over at his bedroom door that I saw it was ajar. When I approached it, and peeked inside I realized that his bed was made. I have no idea if he even made it home last night.

"You're going to sleep with him," she says matter-of-factly. "You're a beautiful woman. He's a smoking hot guy. You're both unattached. It only makes sense that you'd fall into bed together at some point."

I was on the verge of telling her about my impromptu dinner with Sebastian last night but now I push back the urge to share. It will just add to her delusion that it's only matter of time before I hook up with my roommate.

There was definitely something in the air between us at Calvetti's but once I got home and had a hot shower, reality swept over me again.

I have no doubt that a hookup with Sebastian would be mind blowing but when the dust settles, we would be forced to face the fact that Maya and Julian are central parts of our lives.

I don't want to put myself in a position where I run into an ex lover at every family gathering and since Sebastian is like a brother to Julian, that's a real and uncomfortable possibility.

"We're not going to sleep together." I shake my head. "This is a strictly platonic relationship. He rents a room from me. End of story."

A loud laugh bubbles out of her. "If you think that's the end of your story, you're in for the surprise of your life."

I arch a brow. "Oh, really?"

"The sparks between you two the other day were obvious, Tilly. I saw the way he was looking at you. Sebastian Wolf wants you. "

"He doesn't." I scoff.

She stands. "Don't be afraid to have fun. People can sleep together and part as friends. I've done it with men."

I've tried to do it.

It's never worked for me.

Sebastian and I are destined to be roommates, nothing more.

"Let's go to Matiz Cosmetics." She picks up her purse. "A new lipstick color can change a woman's life."

I laugh as I walk toward the kitchen. "My life is good the way it is."

"Says the woman who hasn't had sex in months."

"I'm going to need a reminder of why we're best friends." My lips twitch as I try not to smile. "Speaking of reminders…it's been how long since you slept with a man?"

She runs her hand through her hair. "This is why we need to go on a shopping spree. We need to stop thinking about men, and start thinking about ourselves."

"I'm all for that," I say as I reach for my purse and my coat. "Matiz awaits."

Chapter 14

Sebastian

I breathe a heavy sigh of relief as I slide the key into the lock of the apartment. I've been home twice since I had dinner with Matilda. Both times it was for a four-hour stretch in the middle of the night.

I clocked in three-and-a-half hours of sleep followed by a shave, a shower and breakfast before dawn broke.

On Saturday morning I was surprised when I opened the refrigerator to find an assortment of fruit and vegetables. I grabbed two apples and an orange, then left the apartment mindful of the fact that Matilda was fast asleep in her bedroom.

I did the same this morning. The only difference was the bunch of bananas sitting atop the counter.

She'd been to the grocery store twice in as many days to pick up food for us. I appreciated it and told her as much in a note that I left on the counter.

I was tempted to text her to thank her, but I didn't want to wake her at four a.m., even though seeing her face was what I've craved all weekend while I worked this case.

"Did you catch the bad guy?"

Her voice is like liquid sunshine as it washes over me when I step into the foyer.

I look to where she's sitting on the sofa, her knees curled up to her chest. She's wearing a blue T-shirt and faded jeans with holes in the knees. Her feet are bare. As is her face.

I've never seen a more striking woman without a stitch of makeup on.

"We caught him," I say as I pocket my keys. "It took all fucking weekend, but he's downtown in lock up."

"Is he the one who killed that woman in the park?" Her brows perk as I walk closer to her. "It's been all over the news since Friday night."

"That's the one, " I reply as I lower myself to sit on the corner of the wooden coffee table. "I'm beat. How has your weekend been?"

Her eyes drift from the mindless chatter that's taking place on the television screen to my face. "Fine. Quiet."

Her phone buzzes next to her and a flash of a text message pops onto the screen. Her gaze falls to it before she fishes it into her palm.

"I need to get ready." She shifts in place, stretching her legs. "I'm heading out."

She must have a date.

I don't welcome the unwanted wave of disappointment that washes over me. My plan since I boarded the subway to come home was to shower and then pass the fuck out in my bed.

I know she's due back at work tomorrow so I assumed she'd have a low-key evening planned. Apparently, I assumed wrong.

"I won't wait up," I quip.

She pushes herself up to her feet. "Don't take this the wrong way, but you look dead tired and that's not a lame attempt at a homicide detective joke."

I laugh. "So I look like shit?"

Her gaze glides over my face. "No. I didn't say that."

The inference is there. I know she thinks I'm attractive. I saw the way she was looking at me in the Uber on our way to Calvetti's the other night.

I couldn't take my eyes off of her during dinner. She noticed my interest. I know she did.

I may be exhausted but I'd give up sleep for a week to spend the night continuing the conversation we were having at the restaurant. I want to keep her glued to the spot she's standing for as long as I can, so I ask a question I have no right asking. "Do you want to run the name of the guy you're meeting by me? It wouldn't hurt to double check that he's not a part of an open homicide investigation."

I want her to correct me and tell me she's on her way to see, Kate, the woman I met the day after I moved in.

She shifts on her bare feet. "This one checks out. I've known him for awhile."

Him.

Fuck.

I rub my chin. I'm irritated that it bothers me that she's meeting a guy. I have no claim on her. She's my roommate. That's it.

"I better get going," she says softly. "I'm glad you solved the case. You make the city a safer place."

She sounds like the police commissioner when he leads a press tour through the squad room. "I'll see you soon, Matilda."

Her eyes catch mine for a brief second. "Good night."

I'd wish her the same, but I don't want her to have a good night with anyone else. I want her to stay here with me, but since that can't happen I watch as she walks away before I head straight to my bedroom alone.

Chapter 15

Tilly

"Will you marry me, Tilly?"

I smile as I look over at him. "You've asked me that question three times this weekend, Coop. My answer hasn't changed."

Cooper Gallo's mouth dips into a frown. "The answer is still no?"

I crouch down until I'm almost eye level with the six-year-old. "One day when you're older, you'll meet someone who will steal your heart away. When that happens, you'll be happy that I said no."

"What if it's you?" His small hand rests on my cheek. "If I'm older and you don't have a husband yet, will you marry me then?"

"Why don't we make a pinky swear promise to always be friends? I could use a really good friend like you, Coop."

His pinky on his left hand juts out. "I like that. Let's do it."

I wrap my finger around his gently. "We solemnly swear that we'll always be friends."

"We do," he affirms with a sharp nod of his head.

His blue eyes catch mine. "You're the best babysitter I ever had. Can we look on my mom's laptop at more stuff about the moon?"

I glance over at the clock hanging on the kitchen wall. "We can do that for twenty minutes and then you'll have to get into bed. There's school tomorrow."

"You sound like mom." He giggles. "Can we call her so I can say goodnight to her?"

Even though his mom, Carolyn, left their apartment less than an hour ago, I know how important it is to Cooper to hear her voice before he falls asleep.

When Carolyn started working at Premier Pet Care as a veterinarian she kept mainly to herself. I didn't know she had a son until she brought Cooper to work one day last summer when her nanny was a no-show.

Coop and I hit it off right away. I spent part of my shift with him in the break room. We discovered our mutual love for science and ever since, whenever Carolyn has been in a pinch for a sitter, I've stepped in.

She's a single mom with a demanding career and an ex-husband in another state. I see the stress she's under on a daily basis.

Her new nanny is great, but she came down with the flu two days ago.

Since Carolyn is on call at the clinic this weekend, she sent out a group text yesterday afternoon to all of her New York City contacts. She was looking for someone willing to watch Coop if a pet emergency came up that needed her attention.

I offered immediately since I knew the reassurance of having someone in place to watch her son would take that load off her shoulders.

This is the second time I've been at their apartment since then.

"We'll try and call her right before bed." I watch as he settles into a dining room chair. "If she's busy, we'll leave her a voice message, but I know she'll try her best to answer."

His gaze slides from the laptop screen to my face. "I heard you and mom talking last night before you went home."

I move to where he's sitting. Carolyn and I are friends. We don't hang out after hours because her time is devoted to Coop, but at work we regularly share coffee breaks. She's confided in me about her painful divorce and I've shared horror stories about my search for Mr. Right. We've formed an unlikely bond.

"What were we talking about?" I sit in the chair next to him and reach for the laptop so I can pull up the solar system website he loves exploring.

"I heard you tell mom that you live with a policeman."

I did tell Carolyn that I have a new roommate. I'm grateful now that I didn't mention seeing Sebastian naked.

"I do live with a policeman."

A smile lights up his face. "Does he have a badge?"

I pat my hand over the front of the waistband of my jeans. "He wears it on his belt. I've seen it a couple of times."

"Is it shiny?" His eyes widen.

"It is."

"Cool." His gaze darts to the laptop screen before he looks back at me. "I don't know any policemen. What's his name?"

"Detective Wolf."

His face lights up. "That's the coolest name I've ever heard."

I can't help but laugh. "I guess it's a pretty cool name."

He plays with a button on his pajama top. "Can you bring him with you the next time you come over?"

I hate that I have to be the one to wipe that hopeful expression off his face but I can't exactly ask Sebastian to tag along the next time I babysit. "He's really busy."

"Catching all the bad guys, right?"

"You know it." I smooth my hand over the top of his head.

He turns to look up at me. "You're the luckiest person in the world, Tilly. You get to live with a real life hero."

"I am very lucky." I smile softly. "I get to live with a real life hero and you're one of my best friends."

"We're both lucky, aren't we?" he asks through a toothy grin. "Can we call my mom now?"

His smiles are like sunshine. "You bet. I know nothing makes her happier than hearing your voice."

He's up on his feet racing to where I left my cell phone before I can get in another word.

Chapter 16

Tilly

I look up when I hear the door to Sebastian's bedroom open. I didn't expect to see him this morning. I didn't get home until close to midnight last night.

Carolyn had to perform emergency surgery on a poodle, so after I tucked Cooper into bed, I settled on her sofa with a bag of potato chips and a can of soda. By the time I finished watching a movie, I'd eaten the entire bag of chips. I dusted the crumbs off my jeans and shirt and when Carolyn finally got home, I filled her in on Coop's bedtime request.

He wanted me to tell her he loved her one last time before I left.

I did.

Her eyes welled with tears and I hugged her.

She hasn't had it easy, but she's a fighter and her son adores her. It's obvious that's what keeps her going.

"Good morning." Sebastian steps into the hallway wearing a pair of jeans and a black sweater.

"You're not going to work are you?"

"That's how I pay my share of the rent." He smiles. "I take it you're heading to work too?"

I look down at the blue scrubs I'm wearing. It's the required uniform of every vet assistant who works at Premier Pet Care. "What was your first clue, detective?"

He laughs. "I like that look on you."

I can't tell if it's a genuine compliment, so I ignore it in favor of my original question. "You worked all weekend. Don't you get at least one day to recover from that?"

"My lieutenant doesn't seem to think so." He waves his cell phone in the air. "She called me twenty minutes ago. No rest for the weary."

He may be joking, but I see the exhaustion in his face. I deal with death on a daily basis at the clinic. I know how draining it is.

What he does for a living is on an entirely different level. There's no way it doesn't eat at his core.

"How was your date?" he asks as he pours himself a glass of juice. "I didn't hear you come in."

I didn't correct him about my plans last night because I saw no reason to. I was in a rush to get to Carolyn's and he looked about ready to fall asleep where he was sitting.

"Last night I learned that shadows are darker on the moon and I was proposed to."

He waits for a beat before he responds. "Proposed to?"

"By the six-year-old son of one of the vets I work with." I run my fingertip over the edge of the counter. "Cooper is his name. He's a great kid."

"Smart too," he offers with a smile.

"Carolyn, Cooper's mom, was called into the clinic for an emergency, so I hung out at her place."

"Learning about the moon?" He finishes his juice.

"Anything related to the solar system." I glance over at the microwave to check the time. "Last night it was all about the moon."

"I know the fascination. My parents got me a telescope for my seventh birthday."

"Really?"

"Don't look so surprised." He crosses his arms over his chest. "I'd camp out on the rooftop of our building on clear nights to stargaze."

"So you already knew that shadows are darker on the moon?" I study him, taking in how striking he looks when he's edging toward a smile.

"I did. I also know that the surface of the moon is hot during the day and cold at night. That's common knowledge though, so I'm sure you've heard that before."

I shake my head. "I didn't know that."

He reaches to open the fridge door so he can peer inside. "The next time you see Cooper ask him if he knows that."

"If I tell Cooper that you're a fan of the solar system, he'll…" I stop myself but not before Sebastian shifts his attention from the fridge to my face.

"He'll what?"

"Nothing." I wave the word away with a swat of my hand in the air.

"You were about to say something, Matilda." His voice lowers. "Tell me what it was."

I exhale softly. "Like I said Cooper is six and is fascinated by a lot of different things. One of them is policemen so when he found out I live with one, well…he asked if I could bring you along the next time I babysit."

The expression on Sebastian's face is impassive. I can't read anything from it, so I keep talking to fill the silence. "I told him you're very busy and besides, he doesn't have any clue that we barely know each other. It was just the ramblings of a six-year-old who is fascinated by shiny badges."

His gaze drops to where his badge is hanging from his belt. "If I'm around the next time you see him, I'd love to come with you to get an introduction."

"You would?" I feel the edges of my mouth curl into a smile. "You're serious?"

He leans his hand against the counter, narrowing the distance between us. "He sounds like a great kid. I already know I'll like him."

"Because he loves the moon as much as you do?" I laugh.

"No." His eyes lock on mine. "Because he asked you to marry him. That tells me the kid is wise beyond his years."

I break the moment when I feel a blush creep over my neck. "He asked me to marry him because I give him licorice before bed."

"You're a rule breaker?"

I nod. "Sometimes."

"Good to know, Matilda," he says in a low deep tone. "That's good to know."

I push a strand of hair back into the messy low bun I crafted after my shower this morning. I flick my tongue over my bare bottom lip, wishing I had applied the new pale pink lipstick I bought at Matiz.

"I need to get to work." He rakes me with a glance. "Take care of yourself today."

"I will," I whisper as he brushes past me toward the apartment door.

I will take care of myself. I'm going to do it right now.

The scent of that man's skin, the look in his eyes and the sound of his voice is all the fuel I need to get myself off before I go to work.

Chapter 17

Sebastian

I close the door of the interrogation room behind me as I exit. I've spent the past four hours trying to get a thirty-two-year-old woman to confess to killing her husband.

I already have all the evidence I believe we need to put her away for the rest of her life, but a confession will seal the deal.

Brant and I tapped out to let a pair of female investigators take a run at the suspect. They're both highly skilled, and I have no doubt that by the end of the night, the district attorney's office will be filing a first-degree murder charge against the demure blonde-haired woman who shoved a knife into her husband's neck while he was fast asleep.

"You heading home?" Brant asks from behind his desk.

"Not yet." I drop into my office chair. I never leave when a suspect is on the brink of a confession. This is my case, and I'll follow through with the necessary paperwork tonight. I don't want there to be any delay once this file is handed over to the district attorney for prosecution.

"I did it."

I look over at Brant. "Did what?"

"Popped the question." He smiles. "Guess what she said?"

"I hope to hell it was yes." I raise my chin. "That grin on your face is giving everything away here, Brant."

His smile only widens. "She cried, Sebastian. Remy cried when I got down on one knee. I couldn't have scripted the night better."

"I'm happy for you," I say genuinely. "Don't fuck it up between now and the walk down the aisle."

"That's happening in the next few weeks."

I look down at my desk and the mountain of paperwork I need to get through tonight. Brant has just as much waiting for him, but the guy is lost back in the moment when his girlfriend said yes.

I should have figured it out hours ago. He wasn't invested in the job today. His mind was somewhere else. Now, I know where.

"What's the rush?" I pick up a pen. "Don't most women need months to plan their wedding day?"

His gaze travels around the squad room. It's late afternoon and a hub of activity at the moment. That doesn't bode well for the commissioner's promise to lower murder rates in Manhattan.

"Can I tell you something?" Brant leans over his desk. "I'll need you to keep it between the two of us for now. I'm not going to the lieutenant with this until I know for sure."

I already know the next words out of his mouth.

I've heard the same preface to a confession from a partner before.

He's on the hunt for a new job. One that doesn't require him to look at dead bodies on a regular basis.

"You have my word I'll keep it quiet," I assure him.

"I'm looking at joining the force in Chicago."

"Chicago?" That surprises me. I was expecting him to tell me that he was transferring to robbery or narcotics. I didn't foresee a move to another state. "Why Chicago?"

"Remy misses her folks." He surveys the room again. "You know what they say about a happy wife makes a happy life."

It's a sacrifice not many men in this room would be willing to make.

"The lieutenant has pull in Chicago." I point at her open office door. "She came up the ranks there before she moved here. Talk to her. She'll be pissed when she finds out you're headed there and you didn't ask for her help."

His gaze follows my hand. "You're not setting me up, are you?"

I shake my head. "Christine's door is always open for a reason, Brant. Get in there and tell her what's on your mind. You owe it to her."

He pushes back from his desk. "The wedding's here in New York, so I expect you to show."

"If you let me know when and where I'll be there." I flip through the stack of papers in front of me.

"You'll bring someone, right?"

I look up. "No plus ones for me."

"Remy will insist." He straightens his suit jacket. "There has to be one woman you're willing to sit next to through the ceremony and dinner."

Matilda.

I could sit next to her for hours, days if need be. I didn't want to leave her this morning, but duty called.

"I'll give it some thought," I reply. "Go talk to the lieutenant about Chicago and then burn through that paperwork on your desk. You're still pulling your load until you walk out this squad room for the last time."

***

"You're fucking kidding me, Julian." I lean back into the worn leather of his sofa. "I came here to decompress and now this?"

"What the hell is your problem?" My closest friend raises a brow. "I just asked you to be my best man. This isn't the reaction I was hoping for."

I listened to Brant talk about his pending wedding and potential move to Chicago less than two hours ago. It means I need to break in yet another new partner. I don't know if I have it in me.

I was on my way home from work when Julian called and asked me to stop by his apartment. I expected Maya to be here, but she's having dinner with Matilda.

I was about to tell Julian that I'd trade places with Maya in a heartbeat and then he threw the best man pitch my way.

He's been engaged to Maya for more than a year. I half-expected the two of them to elope at some point given how busy they both are. Maya's devoted herself full-time to real estate and Julian heads up his family's hotel chain.

"What about Griffin?" I ask because I know Julian must have considered our mutual close friend, Griffin Kent, as a contender to stand next to him when he takes his vows.

"You haven't talked to him?" Julian eyes me from where he's sitting in an armchair.

I shake my head. "Not recently. The last time was two weeks ago."

Griffin's engaged too. It's a running joke that I'm the guy no one wants. My best friends are clueless to the fact that I'm not about to ask a woman to make the unique sacrifices that are expected when you're married to a member of the NYPD.

"His caseload has been brutal." Julian scrubs the back of his neck with his hand. "I thought he'd find some time between court dates to squeeze in a quick call to you."

Griffin's a divorce attorney. His job was his life too until he met his fiancée, Piper Ellis.

"You two are obviously keeping secrets from me." I cast him a look. "Am I not part of the club anymore?"

He laughs. "Griffin's got a favor to ask you too."

"A favor?" I blink. "What favor?"

"A once in a lifetime favor." He glances down at his watch. "All I can say is you're the best man we know."

"For fuck's sake." I laugh. "You're not saying that he's going to ask me to be his best man too, are you? What the hell is this? What if I say no to you both?"

"You won't." Julian tugs his cell from his pants pocket. "You'll say yes to us both."

"You're right." I move to stand. "I hope I get a discount on multiple tuxedo rentals."

He eyes the screen of his phone. "Maya wants us to join her and Tilly for dinner at Axel Tribeca? Are you hungry?"

I ate pizza at the station before I left work, but I'm not about to turn down an invitation to see my roommate outside of our apartment. "Count me in."

Chapter 18

Tilly

"You almost had sex with a murderer?" Maya doesn't even try and keep her voice at an acceptable level. Thankfully, no one seated near us seems to be paying attention to our conversation.

"No," I correct her. "I said that I was considering having sex with a man who I found out was once a potential witness in an attempted homicide investigation."

"Now you're splitting hairs."

I shrug. "What? How is that splitting hairs? He didn't kill anyone, Maya. He may have been in the room when someone died, but that… never mind. It doesn't matter. I saw the light and kicked him out."

"You didn't see the light, Tilly." She takes a sip of her iced water. "Sebastian saved the day. You told me he walked in just in the nick of time."

I swear my sister has selective hearing when it comes to me.

When I met her at this restaurant thirty minutes ago, the first words out of her mouth were about Sebastian. She wanted to know everything that's happened between the two of us since I got back from San Francisco.

I skipped right past seeing him naked to the night he walked in to find Donald sitting on the sofa waiting to take me out to dinner.

"The details don't matter." I run my hand through my hair. "What matters is that I can cross another man off my list."

Her gaze drops to her phone yet again. It's the third time in the past ten minutes. I know as a real estate broker she doesn't clock out at five o'clock the way that I do. She's on call twenty-four hours a day, seven days a week for her clients.

"Do you have any fun work stories to share?" I shift the subject from men to her. I love hearing about Maya's work. It's one of her true passions.

"Since we're celebrating your belated birthday tonight, I asked Julian to come for dinner too." Her lips curve into a smile.

I'm not disappointed. I've never been close to Grant, Frannie's husband, and since I've never had a brother of my own, I've hoped that Julian and I could build a bond that would fill that void in my life.

"Is he on his way?" I glance at the screen of her phone.

"He's walking in now." She gestures to the glass door at the entrance of the restaurant.

I look over expecting to see my future brother-in-law. I do, and as Julian lifts his hand to wave in our direction, I spot the handsome man on his heel.

Dressed as he was this morning, but with a late day shadow covering his jaw, Sebastian Wolf smiles at me and my heart skips a solid beat.

***

"Is business always this brisk?" Sebastian asks after Julian orders a bottle of red wine for the table.

This restaurant just happens to be inside of a Bishop Hotel. That means we'll get extra special service. The staff straightened up the moment they noticed Julian walking toward our table.

"It's been a steady increase since we opened." He reaches for Maya's hand. "Did you ask Tilly yet?"

Ask me what?

Before I get a chance to blurt that question out, Maya pipes up. "Not yet. I thought we could do it together. You ask Sebastian and I'll ask Tilly."

Sebastian clears his throat.

I haven't glanced in his direction since he sat next to me. He's been on my mind all day and after my little self-love fest this morning before work, I feel a tinge of guilt. I used my imagination to picture Sebastian naked again. It's becoming a habit that I doubt I'll be breaking anytime soon.

"I already asked Sebastian," Julian says as he runs the pad of his thumb in a circle over my sister's palm.

Maya's gaze darts from his face to Sebastian's. "You said yes, didn't you? Tell me you said yes."

"Of course I did."

I finally look at him, wondering exactly what the question was.

I'm greeted with a sinfully sexy smile and a cock of his left brow. "Matilda will say yes too."

Yes. Whatever it is, yes.

"Tilly." Maya taps me on the shoulder and I hesitantly turn to look at her.

My sister's eyes are welling with tears. She rarely cries so I know that whatever she's about to say is tugging at her heartstrings.

"What is it, Maya?" I ask softly. "What do you want to ask me?"

"I love you," she starts with a hiccup. "You're my best friend. You know that, right?"

I don't. I always thought Falon Shaw was my sister's best friend mainly because Maya introduced her that way when I first moved to New York.

I nod. "I love you too."

"We're getting married soon." She looks to Julian with a smile before her gaze settles back on my face. "I want you to be my maid-of-honor. I want you to stand next to me when I marry the love of my life."

I feel my bottom lip tremble. "Me?"

"You." She reaches to cup her hand over my cheek. "I talked to Frannie about it this morning. I wanted her to know that I picked you."

"I thought…" I begin before I glance over at Julian. He's smiling. His hands are folded together on the table in front of him. When I look back at Maya, her tears have dried. "I thought you'd ask both of us. Frannie asked us both to stand up for her at her wedding."

"I thought about it, but I want it to be you." She sighs. "We've become so close since you moved here and Frannie totally gets it. Besides, Becca and Jolie are going to be flower girls."

Frannie's daughters will make perfect flower girls.

"Tell me you'll do it." Maya laughs. "You want to do it, right?"

"Of course I'll do it." I throw my arms around her shoulders. "Thank you, Maya. Thank you for picking me."

Chapter 19

Sebastian

I don't know how I made it through that dinner without touching Matilda. She was sitting so close to me and looked so fucking beautiful in that navy blue shift dress she was wearing.

She wore her hair down again. This time it was straightened and the light coating of pale lipstick she put on after we'd finished dessert was a beacon that was luring me to her perfect mouth.

Jesus, I wanted to kiss her when she leaned over and whispered that the chocolate cake was the best thing she'd ever tasted.

I wanted to taste her. Her lips, her skin, her pussy, all of her.

I try to shake off the thought as I sit in our living room now.

We'd shared a taxi with Maya and Julian, which meant I was stuck in the front seat while the three of them piled into the back.

They dropped us at our apartment first with a round of hugs and a promise to meet for dinner again in a couple of weeks to go over wedding plans.

I don't know the first thing about planning a celebration of that magnitude, but I'll do it. I'll sit through any discussion about flowers, caterers and photographers if I can do it with Matilda.

"When did Julian ask you to be his best man?" Matilda's voice comes at me from behind.

I sat down on the sofa as soon as we got home. She took off toward her bedroom muttering something about needing to get out of her dress.

The offer to unzip the back of her dress danced on my lips, but I held back because I know I'd want to touch more of her skin and I can't read if she's feeling the same pull to me as I am to her.

"Right before we got to the restaurant." I glance back to see her approaching.

She's changed into cut-off denim shorts and a pink T-shirt. Her toned legs are on display, her nipples have furled into tight points beneath the fabric of the shirt.

"I was surprised that Maya asked me tonight." She sits in the oversized armchair that faces the sofa. "I thought it would be just another birthday dinner, but it turned into a really special night."

I run my palms over my thighs trying to curb my arousal. "I had a great time."

"Me too," she says softly. "Julian and Maya are so in love, aren't they? You can feel it when you're near them. At least I can."

I don't know what love feels like.

"Have you ever been in love?" I ask before I realize that I don't want to know the answer. I don't want to hear about her feeling anything substantial for another man even though I don't know what the fuck it is that I'm feeling for her.

It feels like lust, a pure carnal need to fuck her.

I close my eyes against the swell of my cock in my jeans.

"Once," she whispers. "It was forever ago."

I glance over at her. She's shifted slightly in her seat, so her legs are now crossed at the knee.

"How long is forever ago?" I lean forward, resting my forearms on my thighs.

"High school." She laughs. "Is it love if you're not even eighteen-years-old?"

I watch her face as I answer. "I think it's love if your heart says it is."

"Mine did." She bows her head. "I thought he would be my forever, but it didn't work out."

I've never felt that with a woman.

"I saw him when I was in San Francisco." She glances over at me. "He dropped by my sister's house when we were having birthday cake."

"You invited him?"

My question surprises her. I see it in the slight perk of her brows. "Frannie's husband, Grant, did. They're friends."

"What's his name?" My throat tightens. None of this is my fucking business, but I can't help myself. I crave the knowledge of who this guy is.

She glances at the window and the lights of the city beyond. "Boyd."

Boyd. I hate the name now.

"What was it like seeing Boyd?" His name snaps off my tongue.

"Strange." She frowns. "I hadn't seen him since Frannie's wedding."

Good. I remember Julian telling me that Frannie has been married for years.

"We talked briefly at the birthday party." She looks down at her fingernails. "It was mostly about his job, my job, the weather here versus there. It was just a lot of random shit."

I laugh. "Sounds exciting."

Her lips curl into a smile. "It was boring and it made me wonder what I saw in him all those years ago. There wasn't a spark there anymore."

I feel my body relax. "So Boyd is a bore?"

She catches the corner of her bottom lip with her teeth. "A big bore. He's not my type at all anymore."

I ask because it's right there, dangling like a hook in front of me. "What's your type, Matilda?"

She starts to blush, her hand jumping to her chest. "What's your type?" she counters just as her phone starts ringing next to her.

I toss my head back into the sofa and close my eyes.

Fuck. Just fuck.

"It's Frannie," she says softly. "She wants to video chat. I'll take it in my room."

I don't respond because I was about to tell her that she's my type and then her damn phone rang. Matilda Baker is exactly the type of woman I want in my bed.

She's the only woman I want in my bed.

Chapter 20

Tilly

"Why the frown, you clown?" Frannie laughs at her joke.

I shake my head at the camera on my phone. "That's about as funny now as it was when you first said it. We were eight-years-old then, Fran."

"Maya just asked you to be her maid-of-honor." She tilts her head. "I thought you'd be crying."

"I'm happy." I nod. "I'm excited too."

"You'll do a great job." She tugs the strap of her sundress up until it's sitting on her shoulder. It slips down almost instantly. "It's important to Maya that you stand beside her when she marries Julian. I'm going to be the flower girl wrangler."

I laugh. "I heard. Are the girls excited?"

"Jolie is. Becca is too young to understand." She sighs. "I got my period today."

When I was in San Francisco, Fran made a point of telling me on a daily basis about her desire to have another baby. She loves children. It's obvious whenever I see her with her daughters.

"I'm sorry." I look directly into the camera. "I know today must be hard for you."

A soft smile touches her lips. "It is, but it's not meant to be yet."

Both of her pregnancies were surprises. Now that she's focused and actively trying, it's not happening. This is the third month in a row she's called me with the news that a new baby isn't on its way.

I pause when I hear the unmistakable squeak of the loose floorboard in the foyer followed by the sound of the apartment door closing. That means Sebastian left. I look up at the top of my phone's screen at the time. It's almost midnight.

"I should get to bed soon, Frannie," I lie. I won't be able to sleep. I'm still thinking about the conversation I was having with Sebastian before this call interrupted me.

He was about to tell me what type of woman he's attracted to. I had braced myself for him to say redheads since I know he fucked Wendy, but I imagine his type varies depending on what he's in the mood for.

When his leg brushed mine during dinner, I felt a shiver run through me. I glanced at him, but his gaze was locked on a woman sitting at the bar near the restaurant's entrance.

She was blonde with long legs and shoes that cost more than I make in a year.

Maybe he's on his way back there now.

"Tilly?" Frannie's voice cuts through my thoughts. "You've got something on your mind. What is it?"

"Sleep." I manage a small laugh. "I have to be at the clinic bright and early."

She eyes me with skepticism. "You're lying, but I'm going to let you off the hook because I can see that you're tired."

I'll take the insult if it means I can end the call.

"Good night, Frannie." I smile into the camera. "Sweet dreams."

She blows me a kiss. "'Night, Tilly."

***

"I always knew you were trouble," Dr. Hunt says from where he's standing in the doorway of the break room.

I'm just finishing my lunch which consists of a peanut butter and jelly sandwich I made in a rush this morning before work.

I pressed the snooze button twice before I rolled out of bed and into a warm shower.

Once I was dressed in my scrubs and I'd finished braiding my hair, I went into the kitchen with the hope that I'd see Sebastian.

He wasn't there and his bedroom door was wide open. He either didn't make it home last night or he left before the crack of dawn.

Either way, I felt a stab of disappointment as I poured my morning coffee into a travel mug to take with me.

"What did I do now?" I smile at my boss.

Donovan Hunt has been good to me. He gave me this job right after I landed in New York City. Sometimes I have to work long hours, but the pay is excellent and the benefit is that I get to spend all day with one of the most respected veterinarians in the city. It doesn't hurt that he's a handsome and kind man.

"You tell me." He jerks his thumb toward the waiting room. "There's a police detective here to see you."

"Sebastian Wolf?" My heartbeat quickens when I say his name.

"That's the one." Donovan nods. "I take it you didn't rob a bank. This is a personal visit?"

"It is," I say quietly.

"I thought so." He laughs. "The guy had a smile as wide as the ocean on his face when he asked for you."

I bow my head to hide the blush I feel blooming on my cheeks. "I'll be right out."

He turns to leave. "It's good to see you happy, Matilda."

It's good to feel happy. I brush my hands over the front of my scrubs and follow Donovan out the door.

Chapter 21

Tilly

I see Sebastian immediately when I walk into the waiting room. He's standing next to the reception desk. He's still wearing the same clothes he was last night. His jaw is now covered with day-old stubble. He looks amazing.

"Matilda," he says my name as he sees me approaching. "I'm sorry for bothering you at work."

"No." I shake my head slightly. "It's not a bother at all."

It's more of a thrill actually; at least my nipples and other parts of me feel that way.

"I'm on my way home." He exhales. "I got caught up in a case last night."

I drifted off to sleep thinking he'd gone back to Axel Tribeca to bed the blonde with the killer shoes. I feel a sense of relief knowing that he was at work.

He looks around the packed waiting room. "You're actually one of the reasons for the new lead I was working overnight."

"Me?" My hand darts to the center of my chest.

"I've been trying to track down a witness to a case for weeks." He rakes his hand through his hair. "She got spooked and went into hiding. Apparently, she came out because I spotted her sitting at the bar at Axel Tribeca last night."

He has to be talking about the blonde I thought he was checking out.

"I'm happy to help," I say jokingly. "Did you come down here to tell me that?"

"No. I brought you something."

My gaze drops to his hands and the small white paper bag he's holding. "What is it?"

"Cake." He pushes it toward me. "Chocolate cake. It's from Axel Tribeca. Maya ate most of the piece you ordered last night so I thought I'd pick up a slice just for you. You don't have to share this with anyone."

My hands tremble as I take the bag from him. He can't know how much his words mean to me. How much this gesture means.

"Thank you," I say softly. "You didn't have to do this."

"I was passing the hotel and thought of you." He leans his hip against the reception counter. "Promise me you won't share it. You'll savor every bite yourself."

My eyes lock with his and I feel a rush of energy I've never felt before. "I promise."

"I'll see you tonight."

"I'll see you then," I manage in a small voice. "Thank you again."

His eyes linger on my lips. "It was my pleasure, Matilda."

My heart pounds in my chest as I watch him walk out of the clinic, wishing that I were going home to bed with him.

***

"I need an umbrella," I mutter as I race across the wet sidewalk toward my apartment building.

The cold snap we had has given way to spring-like weather. When I left my place this morning I didn't even bother to grab a jacket. What I could really use right now is an umbrella.

I slide my hand over my hair as I charge into the vestibule of my building. I took the subway home, but the one block walk from the station was enough to make me feel and look like a drowned rat. I got a good glimpse of my reflection in the windows of the building next to mine.

I curse under my breath hoping that Sebastian won't be standing in the main living area when I walk in. I want to duck into my bedroom, take a warm shower and get into dry clothes before I face him.

"Tilly, you look like you could use a towel." Junior, the doorman, says as he spots me from across the lobby. "I have a stock of umbrellas for residents. All you had to do was ask for one on your way out this morning."

I should point out that Junior didn't even bother opening the door for me when I left earlier. He was so engrossed in a phone call with someone named Sasha that he only offered up a weak wave and a nod of his chin as I passed by.

"I'll keep that in mind for next time." I look toward the elevator. "I'm going to head up. It's been a long day."

"Your new roommate is a cop."

I turn and look at him. Junior is at least twice my age, with graying temples and fine lines around his eyes. His face is friendly even when it's not sporting a smile as it is now. "I know that."

"I didn't know until ten minutes ago when he walked past me and I saw his badge."

My heart drops.

"Was he on his way in or out?" I ask expectantly.

"Out." He gestures toward the street. "He was in a rush. There must be something going down."

An image of Sebastian going down on me pops into my head.

Shit. I don't need to think about that while I'm staring at Junior's face.

"Isn't there always something happening in this city?" I quip. "I need to dry off. Enjoy your night, Junior."

"You too, Tilly." He taps the brim of his hat. "I hope it's a night to remember."

It may be his standard line, but I was truly hoping for a night to remember. Now that Sebastian has gone to work, my night will consist of a bubble bath and frozen pizza.

All it will be is forgettable.

Chapter 22

Sebastian

There's no way in hell I'm ever going to forget this night.

I stand in the foyer of the apartment staring at the sight in front of me. Matilda doesn't realize I'm here. If she did, she wouldn't be perched on the top of the dining room table with her back to me in nothing but a pair of black lace panties and a bra.

Music is blaring from a mini speaker on the kitchen counter. Her ass is swaying to the beat.

It's obvious from my vantage point that she's changing a light bulb in the chandelier that hangs over the table.

I'll never again look at a light fixture the same way.

Her curvy ass is perfection.

I want to touch it, bite it. *Fuck it.*

My cock hardens instantly.

I need to tell her I'm here. It's the right thing to do. The wrong thing would be to open my jeans, palm my dick and pump one out to the vision in front of me.

I close my eyes against the urge.

"Oh my God," Matilda screams. "Sebastian, oh no."

My eyes pop open to the sight of her turned right around, her hands desperately trying to cover her body.

Jesus. I think I could come just from looking at her.

Turn around, asshole. Turn the fuck around.

I listen to the demanding voice in my head that is telling me to do the right thing. I pivot on my heel so I'm not facing her anymore.

"I'm sorry," I say loudly. "I just walked in."

"I'll turn the music down."

She shuts it off and the sudden silence echoes through me. I can hear her ragged breathing. Or is it mine?

I'm so aroused. The need to fuck is there. I rake my hands through my hair to try and quiet the want.

I hear her footsteps as she pads across the hardwood.

"You scared me," she whispers from behind me. "You said in your text that you'd be at work all night."

I expected to be.

Brant called me hours ago to say that the woman I spotted at Axel Tribeca last night had finally decided to give a statement. I traded the T-shirt I was wearing for a blue dress shirt and a black suit jacket and took off. By the time I got down to the station, she was wavering again.

It took hours and endless negotiation between her lawyer and the district attorney's office to reach an agreement that granted her immunity from prosecution in exchange for her testimony.

My gaze skims the watch on my wrist. "It's almost one, Matilda. I thought you'd be fast asleep by now."

I feel her fingers brush against my shoulder. "You can turn around."

I do.

Her soft smile is the first thing I see. Her chestnut hair is tumbled in waves around her shoulders. The faux fur blanket I wrapped around myself the first night we met is now draped around her small frame. She's breathtaking.

"I broke my own rule." She closes her eyes briefly. "I'm sorry for that."

I inhale deeply. The scent of her skin is intoxicating. "You don't need to apologize to me."

That draws her brows together. "I guess we are even now."

Like fuck we are. She saw my cock. I want more of her body. I want to see her beautiful tits and the pussy that I crave.

I swallow hard, suppressing the need to push for more. "You could say that."

"Thanks again for the salad," she effortlessly changes the subject.

I'd started to make us dinner when I got the call from Brant. I put the salad I'd prepared into the fridge and left. An hour later, I sent Matilda a text telling her to eat it for dinner since I'd be at work all night.

She sent me back a quick thank you message.

"I hope it was better than the candy bar I had for dinner in the squad room."

Her gaze searches mine. "Do you ever get tired of it?"

I wait for a beat before I respond even though I know exactly what she's referring to. Almost everyone in my life has asked me the same question at some point. "Tired of what?"

The blanket slips down her shoulder to reveal a thin black bra strap. "Your job. I don't know how you do it."

I glance at the ceiling to try and tame my raging hard-on before she notices. "Some days are harder than others."

"Was today hard?"

I shake my head. "It was easy."

"What made it easy?" she asks quickly in response.

"I was working an older case." I run my hand over my jaw. "It's the new ones that kick the shit out of me."

"New? You mean when you're called out to a murder and you have to solve the case by starting at square one?"

She makes it sound like a board game or a puzzle. I wish it were that easy. "The worst is the notifications. My lieutenant told me that it would get easier with time, but it's only gotten harder."

Her blue eyes widen. "When I first started at the vet clinic, I was the one who had to stand next to the family members when the doctors told them that their pets weren't going to make it or had passed away."

She clears her throat before she continues, "I'm not saying it's the same, but I cried every time. I still break down if I'm in the room when they hear the news. There's no way I could handle it all the time like some of the other vet assistants."

I'm not surprised. Her heart is too soft, too open, and too compassionate to deal with death on a daily basis.

"You have a kind heart, Matilda."

"Do you really think that's true?" She inches one of her bare feet forward.

"Without a doubt." My eyes glide over her beautiful face.

She parts her lips before taking a deep breath. "You have a kind heart too. You're not the arrogant jerk I thought you'd be."

Smiling, I cross my arms over my chest. "Is that so?"

She nods softly. "You're a good man, Sebastian."

I lean forward so my breath skirts over her forehead. "What makes you say that?"

She looks up and into my eyes. "You make me feel special."

Chapter 23

Tilly

I must be delirious from a lack of sleep. I just told Sebastian he makes me feel special.

He hasn't said a word, so I rush to clarify. "I mean I've never had a roommate who worried about what I was eating, or who brought me cake at work."

His gaze slides over my face. "We're more than just roommates."

I inhale sharply. "We are?"

"We're friends." His mouth curves into a broad grin. "You consider us friends, don't you?"

I hadn't thought about that. We only met a short time ago, but it feels like I've known him for years. That has to be because Maya has mentioned Sebastian to me dozens of times since she met Julian.

"I think we're friends," I whisper back. "Yes, we're friends."

He nods. His face is so close to mine that I'd only need to edge forward a few inches to brush my lips against his.

"I have a feeling that you know a lot more about me than I know about you." A smile ghosts his mouth.

"I doubt that. Maya loves to talk. I'm sure she filled you in on every detail there is to know about me."

His eyes drop to the skin on my chest that is exposed. The top of my bra is visible, but I don't move to adjust the blanket. "She didn't. I know the bare essentials. You're twenty-five, a vet assistant, you like chocolate cake and dancing on dining room tables in the middle of the night."

"I wasn't dancing." The rapid beating of my heartbeat echoes in my ears. "I was changing a light bulb that had burned-out."

His gaze slides from my face to the chandelier before he locks eyes with me. "Let me rephrase. I know you like dancing on dining room tables while you're changing light bulbs."

He saw me in the lingerie I bought when I was in San Francisco. I'd put it on after my shower because it was new. I left it on because I loved the way it made my body look. I had no idea that Sebastian would see me in it too.

"I'm not complaining," he goes on. "You're a great dancer."

I laugh. "I like listening to music when I'm home alone. That was one of my favorite songs."

"Mine too." He rubs the pad of his thumb over his bottom lip. "I try to keep my dancing reserved to solid ground though."

I stare at the movement of his thumb. "What fun is that?"

"Maybe we'll try it together sometime and you'll see." His hand drops to his side and I keep my gaze pinned to his lips.

They must be incredible to kiss. They're full and look so soft.

A loud clap of thunder startles us both. I take a step back and his eyes dart to the windows in the living room.

"It sounds like the rain is back," I say softly.

He checks his watch. "It's late. Do you work tomorrow?"

I nod. "Nine o'clock sharp."

Whatever moment we had was stolen by the approaching storm. I see it in his eyes before he speaks. "We should probably call it a night. I've got an early morning too."

I tug the blanket closer to my body. "Good night, Sebastian."

He only nods in response before he looks back at the window and the raindrops now beating against it.

***

"Why were you changing a light bulb in your lingerie?" Kate forks a piece of chicken from her leftover stir-fry.

When she texted me this morning to invite me to meet her for lunch at her store, she told me that she'd ordered too much take-out last night and the only thing I needed to bring with me was my appetite.

I sat down in a chair next to her desk ten minutes ago and I'm already filled to the brim with ginger beef and vegetables.

"I put on the lingerie after I had a shower." I sigh. "I had a robe on most of the night, but then I went to bed. I couldn't sleep so I got up to listen to some music and I noticed a burned-out light bulb, so I decided to change it."

"Lucky Sebastian." She wiggles her brows. "I can't believe he saw you in nothing but a bra and panties."

It was the first thing I told her when we started eating. It was enough to cause her to almost choke on a piece of broccoli.

"It was karma for me seeing him without any clothes the night we met," I say matter-of-factly.

That draws a laugh from her. "That's not karma. That's fate."

I shrug. "Whatever it was it felt like magic to me. I swear something was happening between us."

"So you're ready to admit that I was right?" She puts her fork down. "You can see that the man wants you, can't you?"

If she had asked me that early this morning when I was standing toe-to-toe with Sebastian in our apartment, my answer would be a resounding *yes*. Since I woke up I've started questioning whether I was reading too much into what was going on between us when he got home from work.

"He was flirting," I admit. "That much I know for sure."

"Call it what you want." She reaches for a paper napkin. "I call it a prelude to a fuck. You two are going to sleep together soon. Mark my words, Tilly."

I pick up my chopsticks. "That's a huge conclusion to jump to. We are so far from that right now. It's not even close, Kate."

"It's the distance from your bedroom to his. That's all it is."

With that, she dives back into eating her lunch and I do the same, the entire time wondering if Sebastian is thinking about me as much today as I am about him.

Chapter 24

Sebastian

"You stood me up again, Sebastian." Darrell Carver pats me on the back as we exit the courtroom. "It's the third time in two months. I'm beginning to wonder if you're just not that into me."

I huff out a laugh as I look back over my shoulder at him. "You can blame work for the missed beers."

I slow as we near the elevators in the corridor. "I'm done here, right? I can head back to the squad room?"

"I won't be calling you back to the stand." He glances over at the attorney representing the defendant in the attempted murder case he's currently prosecuting.

I was on Darrell's witness list. It's part of the job. I stopped by his office for a brief visit before court was in session to go over my testimony.

I recalled the facts of the night of the attack and the investigation as I remembered them when I took the stand. The defendant's attorney tried her best to poke holes in my statements. She failed.

"How's work treating you?" he asks as we wait side-by-side for the elevator.

"The same as always." I shrug.

He turns on his heel, so he's facing me. "Listen, Sebastian. I've got this buddy. He's a friend-of-a-friend of the Dean of Admissions at NYU Law School."

I raise my hand in the air. "Stop right there, Darrell. We've gone over this."

"Hear me out." He looks at the two men standing next to us before he lowers his voice. "I can put in a good word for you if you apply again. I'm not saying I'd have any pull as to whether you're accepted or not, but it wouldn't hurt for me to reach out to sing your praises."

My jaw tightens. "There's no need."

"You owe it to yourself to at least consider it. We both know you'd make a hell of a prosecutor."

The elevator dings its arrival just in time. I turn to the doors waiting for them to open. "I had my chance. That's a part of my past."

"Fair enough." He raises his hands in the air. "I should warn you that I'm going to push you on this the next time we meet for beers."

I take a step back as two women exit the elevator once it opens. "Thanks for the heads-up."

He smiles. "I'm just looking out for a friend."

I don't tell him I appreciate it, although I do. I'm a cop. There has always been a Wolf on the force. That duty fell on my shoulders. I can't walk away from it now.

***

I press my palms against my eyes, desperately trying to will away the image of Matilda dancing on the table last night in her lingerie. It's been a constant in my mind all day, even during court this morning.

"A migraine?" Liam asks from across the table in the diner he asked me to meet him at for lunch.

I drop my hands. "No. I'm fine."

"You're far from fine." He looks over the menu. "You've got something on your mind. Spill it, Sebastian."

I'm not about to tell my youngest brother what happened last night. He'll ask me how I feel about it and I have no fucking clue.

"Have you heard from Nicholas recently?" I resort to a question about one of the few things we have in common, our brother, Nicholas.

Nicholas is older than Liam but younger than me.

He's also one of the world's premier novelists. His series of detective mysteries has sent his star into the stratosphere.

He's currently on a book tour in Europe with his wife, Sophia, and his daughter, Winter Rose.

"Yesterday," he admits. "They're having a blast. He asked about you."

Of course, he did. Nicholas has always had a sixth sense when it comes to me. He can look at me and tell when something is off. I've been avoiding his calls recently only because the last conversation we had before he boarded the flight to Paris was a rough one.

Nicholas is convinced that I'm sacrificing too much for the job.

Since he married Sophia and became a dad, he's been on a crusade to enlist Liam and me in the happily-married-family-man club.

Liam is sure as hell not ready for that.

Marriage and kids don't go with my career choice.

"How's it going with your new roommate?" He sets the large menu down in front of him on the table. "Did you apologize for flashing your dick in her direction?"

"I did." I pat my hand on the wooden table. "She accepted my apology and we've moved on."

He narrows his eyes. "Moved on? What exactly does that mean?"

I tell the truth as Matilda and I established it last night. "We're friends."

"Friends?" He draws the word out. "With benefits?"

I shake my head. "Just friends."

"You're good with that?" He looks over at the blonde server who hasn't taken her eyes off of him since we walked in.

"Why wouldn't I be?"

"I doubt like hell I could live with a beautiful woman and not let my mind drift to all the what-ifs." He drinks from the water glass in front of him.

"I didn't say my mind hasn't wandered." I laugh. "The dynamic is complicated. She's Julian's family. I'm his best friend. There's a line there that's becoming blurrier by the day."

"You're all adults, Sebastian. You don't need Julian's approval to do anything. If you're interested in this woman, tell her."

I would if it wasn't for the guilt that gnaws at my gut when I think about the inevitable conversation between Julian and me when Matilda realizes I'm not the Prince Charming she's looking for.

I know I'm a great fuck, but beyond that, I can't offer her what Julian's giving to Maya.

She deserves better than a man who is married to his job.

He steals another glance at the server. "I'm about to order. You ready?"

"You're about to ask for her number."

He laughs as he shakes his head. "I have it. Our relationship is professional."

"I take it she's not a colleague, so she's a patient?"

"I can't answer that."

I look over at the young woman. She must be a patient. I sense the sadness that's surrounding her.

"I'm proud of you," I say in a low voice. "You're making a difference in the world, Wolf."

He smiles at the nickname I gifted him with when he was a kid. "I'm proud of you too. Don't tell Nicholas but you're my favorite brother."

I shake my head. "When's the last time you said the same thing to him?"

"Yesterday," he says as he raises his hand to beckon the server to our table.

I chuckle under my breath. "Why am I not surprised?"

Chapter 25

Tilly

I zip up the white sweater I pulled off the floor of my closet after I slipped into a pair of faded jeans. I kick a pair of sneakers aside to reveal black leather boots I haven't worn in more than a year.

They'll have to do. I step into those before I tie my hair into a ponytail and twist it into a messy knot on the top of my head.

Done.

I wouldn't say that was a record-breaking change of clothes, but it's fast enough to guarantee that I'll make it to Carolyn's apartment before her date arrives.

I worked an hour late tonight and just as I pushed the key into the lock of my apartment door, my cell phone rang.

It was Carolyn in a panic.

Her nanny had misread the schedule and made plans of her own on the one night this year that Carolyn has a date.

The lucky guy is a sales rep from one of the dog food brands that we stock at the clinic. He caught Carolyn's eye a few weeks ago and when he invited her to dinner and a movie, she happily accepted.

I thumb out a message telling her that I'm on my way before I grab my purse from where I threw it on my bed when I got home from work just minutes ago.

The entire ride home on the subway I imagined walking into the apartment to the smell of a home cooked meal and the sight of Sebastian waiting by the dining room table with two glasses of red wine in his hands and that same look in his eye that I saw last night.

The only thing waiting for me when I did get home was a note taped to the apartment door asking me to keep my music to an *acceptable level* after midnight.

Apparently, I have at least one neighbor who doesn't appreciate pop music the way I do.

I flick the switch to turn off my bedroom light before I race down the hallway to the apartment door.

A chime from my cell pulls my eyes to the screen. It's a reply from Carolyn saying that she appreciates me filling in at the last minute.

I start typing out a message telling her how much I love hanging out with Cooper as I swing the apartment door open. I take a step forward and crash into the hard chest of my roommate.

I look up and into those brilliant blue eyes. "Hey."

"Hey, yourself." Sebastian smiles down at me. "Where are you rushing off to?"

How can he look this good after working all day?

"I need to go watch Cooper." I move to let him into the foyer. "His mom has a date and the nanny bailed."

"Cooper? Is that the kid who loves the solar system almost as much as I do?"

I nod. "I'm going to research more moon facts on my phone on the subway so I can dazzle him with my knowledge."

"Or I could tag along and feed you those facts firsthand." He tugs on the lapel of his gray suit jacket. "Do you think he'd mind?"

I look down at his belt and the badge attached to it. "He'll want to touch your badge."

His gaze drops. "I'll let him hold it."

My heart sings in my chest at the idea of spending an entire evening with Sebastian, even if a six-year-old will steal most of his attention away.

"Cooper is going to love meeting you. I'm pretty sure you're already his hero."

He laughs. "I need to lock something in the safe in my room and then I'll be set."

It's his gun. I catch a glimpse of it in the holster he's wearing under his suit jacket when he moves.

As he walks away, I'm hit with the sudden realization that he puts his life on the line every day.

An unexpected wave of fear washes over me. I've known him for less than a month, but if something happened to him, I know instinctively that my life would never be the same again.

***

"You make the best grilled cheese sandwiches in the entire world," Cooper exclaims as he stands on one of the dining room chairs. "Tilly usually gives me an apple before bed and some licorice. This was way better."

A hint of a smile touches Sebastian's mouth. "My mom taught my brothers, my sister and me how to make grilled cheese when we were a little older than you are."

"What are their names?" Cooper asks as he eyes me.

I'm motioning for him to sit back down in his chair, but he's still on his feet, bouncing in place.

"I have two brothers, Nicholas and Liam."

"What's your sister's name?" He rests his small palms against the table as he stomps his feet on the chair.

"Nikita, but we call her Nyx," Sebastian answers.

I've heard bits and pieces about all of them from Maya. She hasn't met his sister yet, but she had dinner with his two brothers and Nicholas's wife, Sophia, a few months ago.

"I don't have any brothers or sisters." Cooper reaches into the pocket of his sweatpants to pull out Sebastian's badge. "Are any of them policemen like you?"

Sebastian gets up from his chair and goes to where the little boy is standing. He scoops him up effortlessly and tosses him over his shoulder.

Coop lets out a playful squeal.

"My brother, Nicholas, writes books," he says as he walks toward the living room. "My brother, Liam, helps people when they're sad and Nyx owns a candy store."

"A candy store?" Cooper's eyes widen when Sebastian places him down on the sofa.

"The best one in the city." Sebastian takes a seat next to him. "If your mom says it's okay maybe Tilly and I can take you there the next time we come over to hang-out with you."

The next time.

I smile inwardly at the promise of another evening like this.

I've been on my own since we arrived two hours ago. Coop took to Sebastian immediately and they spent most of the evening looking at books and websites devoted to the moon.

I didn't mind at all. I watched in wonder as Sebastian shed his suit jacket, rolled up the sleeves of his white dress shirt and got on the floor so he could read to Cooper.

"I can't wait." Coop pats Sebastian on his knee. "Why aren't any of them policemen like you?"

Sebastian steals a glance back at me before he turns his attention to the inquisitive little boy. "It wasn't what they wanted to do."

"Did you always want to do it?" He looks at Sebastian's face. "Sometimes I think I want to be a pet doctor, but today I think I want to be a detective like you."

I see Sebastian's shoulders tighten. "For a very long time I wanted to be a lawyer."

"What's that?"

Sebastian bows his head. "A lawyer helps the police to make sure that the bad guys go to jail and stay there."

A lawyer? His admission surprises me.

"That sounds cool." Cooper slides into his lap. "Why didn't you do that?"

Sebastian runs his hand over Coop's forehead. "I almost did, but I changed my mind. My dad was a policeman and his dad was too. It made them happy when I went to the police academy."

Cooper looks down at the badge in his hand. "If you were a lawyer you wouldn't have one of these. You can take it back now."

Sebastian reaches toward it, his hand hesitating before he picks it up. "You're right. I wouldn't."

"It's time to get ready for bed," I call from where I'm standing. Something has shifted in Sebastian's demeanor and now is the perfect time to get Cooper tucked in between his sheets. "Say goodnight to Sebastian."

Cooper slides off Sebastian's lap and faces him. "Are we friends now?"

"You bet." Sebastian musses his hair.

"I'm going to tell the kids at school that my best friend is a policeman."

"Hey," I say as I approach where they're sitting. "I thought we were best friends."

Cooper blows out a breath. "You're my second best friend."

I laugh. "I'll take it."

We start toward his bedroom when he stops in place and turns around to look at Sebastian. "I sometimes ask Tilly to marry me, but she always says no. She might say yes if you ask her."

"Cooper," I say his name in a rush. "Sebastian and I are just friends."

He grabs my hand and pulls it toward his bedroom. "Come on. I want you to read me the book about the astronaut."

I glance back at Sebastian. We lock eyes and he smiles softly.

I turn away when Cooper yanks on my hand again. I can't wait to get him into bed so I can spend time alone with the man I think I might be falling for.

Chapter 26

Tilly

"He fell asleep before I got to the third page of the book," I say as I walk back into the main living area of Carolyn's apartment. I reach to pick up toys as I make my way to the sofa where Sebastian is still sitting.

He slides to his feet to help. "He's a great kid, Matilda. He might actually know more about the moon than I do."

I laugh as I pile the toys into a bin in the corner. "Do you want something to drink? Carolyn usually keeps a few cans of soda in the fridge, or I can get you a glass of water."

He dumps the toys he's collected into the bin. "Nothing for me."

"I'll grab something for myself." I start the walk toward the kitchen. "Cooper is going to talk about meeting you for days."

I hear Sebastian chuckle as I round the corner and grab a soda from the fridge. I pour it into a glass. I take a large sip before I head back out toward the living room.

Sebastian is still on his feet, but he's grabbed his cell phone from where he put it on the coffee table earlier.

All evening it's been chiming signals of incoming text messages. I expected him to announce that he had to get back to work, but instead he read the messages without replying.

His fingers are rapidly typing something on the screen now. I don't interrupt. Instead, I cross over to the dining room table, place the glass down, and tidy the books and laptop so it's one less thing Carolyn will have to deal with tomorrow.

I raise my head when I hear Sebastian curse under his breath.

"Is something wrong?" I twist my lips wondering if he's about to walk out because of work.

He looks over at me. I see the hesitation in his expression before he answers. "It's Wendy. She wants to meet for a drink."

I didn't see that coming. I look down to hide the disappointment I know is on my face.

"My mom taught me to be a gentleman at all costs." He lets out a measured breath. "It's not easy to do that when you're trying to end a … when you're trying to tell a woman that the arrangement you had with her is over."

"It's over?" My voice takes on a higher pitch.

Dammit. Why the hell did I ask that question?

A look of satisfaction flashes across his face. "Yes."

My heart does a happy dance inside my chest. I have no idea if Wendy is the only woman he has an arrangement like that with, but she's the one I know he fucked in our apartment.

I'm relieved to know that it won't happen again.

Just as I'm about to invite him to sit with me on the sofa, the apartment door opens and Carolyn walks in.

We both turn to look at her.

The broad grin on her face says it all, but I ask anyway. "How was your date?"

She closes the door softly behind her. "Good, I think. We'll see if he calls for a second date. Thank you both again for taking care of Coop."

"It was our pleasure," Sebastian responds evenly. "You have an amazing son."

"I think so too," she says happily as she pushes her blonde hair back from her forehead. "I hope he behaved."

"He was an angel," I interject. "Hanging out with him is the best."

"You two can take off." She gestures toward the foyer. "The night is still young. Why don't you head to the bar across the street and have a drink?"

I turn on my heel, so I'm facing her. Raising a brow, I tilt my head. "We've both had a long day. I think we'll head home."

"I could use a drink." Sebastian walks across the apartment toward the door. "It was good to meet you, Carolyn."

"You too, Sebastian." She winks at me when I look back at her. "I hope you both have fun tonight."

I shake my head. When we first arrived hours ago, she eagerly shook Sebastian's hand before pulling me aside to ask me why the hell I wasn't sneaking into his bed at night. I laughed it off, but obviously, she's trying to set us up now. "Goodnight, Carolyn."

She leans closer to tug me into an embrace, whispering into my ear, "I really hope you have a sheet-clawing, screaming-at-the-top-of-your-lungs night."

I laugh softly as I pull back. “I’ve never had one of those.”

She looks past my shoulder to where Sebastian is standing. “I think tonight may be the night you do.”

Chapter 27

Sebastian

I head back to the table after picking up two bottles of beer from the bar. Matilda is sitting in the chair nearest the corner staring out the window at the traffic that's passing by.

We were lucky to find a secluded table in this bar. It's packed. Most of the people here are looking for the same thing; a warm and willing body to spend the night with.

I know the drill. It was how I lived my life for many years.

Have a drink, pick up a random woman, and screw her senseless. There was never an exchange of numbers, often not even names.

It served its purpose when I needed it to.

My hookups the last few years have been anchored in casual friendships, like the one I had with Wendy. She was pushing for more time tonight and I realized that seeing her again isn't something I want.

I set one of the beers down in front of Matilda and take the seat next to her. "We should toast to finding an open table."

She laughs as she picks up the bottle and taps it against mine. "Here's to luck and fate."

I take a pull of the beer and place it down. "Tonight was fun. Cooper's a blast."

She sips from her bottle. "It was great. Thanks for tagging along."

I'd follow her just about anywhere at this point. I want her to know that, but I can't read what's running through her mind, so I keep the conversation generic. "So you work with Carolyn?"

"She's a vet." She cups her hand around the bottle. "I'm not always paired up with her during exams or procedures, but we hang out in the break room sometimes."

"Do you like what you do?"

She grins. "I do. The clinic I work at is one of the best in the city. The staff is friendly. We're like a family."

I sense a *but* sitting on the tip of her tongue, so I push. "Is it your dream job?"

She sighs as she takes another swallow of beer. "Are you asking if I want to be a veterinarian?"

Her shoulders tense enough that I can tell it's an unwelcome question that she's been asked too many times in the past.

"I'm asking if you could have any job in the world, would this be it?"

Her eyes widen as she studies my face. "I could ask you the same after hearing you tell Coop that you wanted to be a lawyer."

She's deflecting, but I won't push. "I did want to be a lawyer."

"A prosecutor," she says as she leans closer to look into my eyes. "Eventually the sign on your office door would read Sebastian Wolf, Manhattan District Attorney."

"That was the dream at one time." I pick up the beer but place it down again before taking a drink.

We're talking about a part of me that I've kept close to the vest for years. I could have lied to Cooper when he asked if I always wanted to be a cop, but I didn't see the purpose in that. He's a child. The least he can expect from the adults he interacts with is honesty.

I knew there was a good chance Matilda would bring it up.

"Is it still the dream?" she asks quietly. "Do you still think about becoming a lawyer?"

I rake a hand through my hair. "It crosses my mind from time-to-time."

"Do you ever think about going for it?" She glances over my shoulder toward the bar and the dozens of people gathered there.

"Going back to school?" I chuckle. "I wasn't a model student the first time around."

She bites the corner of her bottom lip. "Can I tell you something?"

"Anything," I whisper as I rest my hand on the table near hers. I want to reach out and scoop it into mine before she makes her confession.

"At least once a week someone asks me if I want to be a veterinarian." She looks down at the table. "Sometimes it's a person who comes into the clinic with their pet. A lot of the men I've dated have asked me. My parents still ask me. It's one of those questions that I'm asked so often that I can sense when it's coming."

I listen intently, sensing that she's exposing a part of herself to me.

"When I was a kid my parents would take my sisters and me to this animal retreat near San

Francisco. It's called the New Springs Pet Retreat." She fingers the zipper on her sweater. "Maya and Frannie didn't get the appeal. They'd pet the animals and beg to go home. I begged to stay."

"You've always loved animals," I state. It's not a question because the answer is obvious.

"My dad is allergic to almost everything." She sighs. "So we could never have a pet of our own, but at New Springs I would spend hours caring for the animals, feeding them, and talking to them. It was my heaven. I spent every single day of my summer vacations volunteering there until I graduated from college."

"That's why you became a vet assistant?" I take a sip of my beer.

"It was the next best thing to my dream job."

"Working at the retreat full-time?" I question with a cock of my brow.

She shakes her head. "Owing it. Running it."

"You can't do that from New York," I point out.

"The couple who owned it when I was a kid sold it three years ago." She runs her fingertip along the surface of the table in a circle. "That was right around the time I graduated. I decided I needed a change, so I moved to New York."

"The point of my very long-winded story…" She huffs out a laugh. "My point is that I had a dream but it fell through, so I found a new dream to be passionate about. I don't need to chase after the obvious brass ring to be fulfilled. I don't want to be a vet. I've never wanted to be a vet. I'm happy standing next to the vets to help them do what they love."

"That's what's important, isn't it?" I ask. "Personal fulfillment?"

"I think so." She shrugs. "Maybe you're not meant to work with the district attorney's office helping them put criminals away. Maybe you're supposed to be in that office getting the job done. If being a detective isn't your backup dream, you owe it to yourself to pursue what you really want."

She's what I really want right now. I look at her gorgeous face. "Do you have any other dreams, Matilda?"

"A few," she says simply. "Do you?"

I stare at her lips. "Many."

"Tell me one," she whispers as she leans even closer.

"I'd rather show you." My voice is husky and low.

Her gaze drops to my mouth as she wets her bottom lip with a swipe of her tongue. "Show me."

I do.

I push every reservation I've had to the side when I wrap my hand around the back of her neck, lean forward and press my mouth to hers for a soft kiss.

Chapter 28

Tilly

I weave my fingers into his hair to deepen the kiss. He groans into my mouth in response and all I want to do is crawl into his lap.

At this moment I don't care about Maya or Julian, any of the people around us, or what happens tomorrow.

Nothing exists but this man and me.

His kiss is everything I imagined it would be. It's tender yet demanding, soft and sensual and the way his tongue flicks over my bottom lip to tempt me to let him in makes my entire body weak.

A loud crash breaks us apart but not before Sebastian trails his lips over my cheek.

I catch his eye for a brief second and I see the same lust I feel reflected back in his gaze.

"For fuck's sake," he says under his breath as he looks over at the bar.

Another even louder crash draws many of the bar's patrons to their feet, including Sebastian. It's obvious from the drunken cheers and litany of curse words filling the air that there's either a fight in progress or one is about to happen.

"You both need to calm the hell down, or I'm going to call the cops." An angry woman's voice rises above the noise.

"I fucking dare you." A man's gruff voice responds.

"I should do something." Sebastian reaches for my hand to draw my knuckles to his mouth. He kisses them softly. "Don't move. I don't want you getting hurt."

I sit in place for a total of ten seconds before I follow behind him. The crowd that's gathered near the bar parts as he pushes his way through.

I watch as he grabs the shirt collar of a man half his size. "What the hell is going on here?"

"I was…I was…I wanted to help her," he stutters as he looks up at Sebastian, his thumb jerking toward the bartender.

"This is none of your business, asshole." Another much larger man steps closer to Sebastian as the smaller man scurries away. The crowd let's out a collective "hell yeah" in response.

"I'm NYPD, so it is my business." Sebastian's hand dips into his pants pocket to tug something out. I assume it's his badge since I saw him slide it in there after Cooper handed it back to him.

"I have one of those too." The obviously drunk man spits out as he runs a hand over his shaved head. "I got it for five bucks from a guy in Times Square. It's a pussy magnet, isn't it?"

Sebastian shakes his head as he pockets his badge and turns to face the man directly. They're the same height, likely the same weight but the man's arms are crossed over his chest in a stance that says he's itching to fight whoever gets in his way.

"Leave now, or I'll arrest you." Sebastian's tone is laced with frustration.

"For what?" The man laughs. "Trying to pick up a woman?"

Sebastian eyes the crowd. "I doubt like hell any woman in here wants anything to do with you so get lost."

A sharp poke to his shoulder sends Sebastian's hands in the air. "Do not touch me."

"Or what?" The man slurs as he jabs his index finger into Sebastian's shoulder again.

"Do you want to spend the night in lockup?"

"I want to beat the shit out of you, pretty boy."

That lures a round of whistles from the crowd. Several people step back giving Sebastian and the man more room.

"I'm giving you one last chance to walk out of here now." Sebastian turns to the bartender. "What's the damage? Did he break anything?"

"A couple of beer bottles and a glass." She shrugs it off from where she's standing behind the bar. "I just want him gone."

"Get out." Sebastian grabs the man by the bicep. "Go home and sleep it off."

My breath catches in my chest when the man spins around and pushes Sebastian back.

His hand lands on the corner of the bar to anchor his stance but not before the man attempts to punch him.

Sebastian darts out of the way warning the man to step back. He does and stumbles.

He recovers quickly and I have to close my eyes the second I see his fist connect with Sebastian's face.

I hear the crowd cheer and when I open my eyes again, the man is pinned to the floor on his chest.

His left arm is twisted behind him in Sebastian's grasp as he reads the drunken bastard his rights.

I catch a glimpse of Sebastian's face when he volleys a gaze in my direction.

Blood is trailing from his nose onto his pristine white shirt. He smiles at me and I feel my breath catch in my throat.

There's no way in hell I'm ever going to forget our first kiss.

Chapter 29

Tilly

I stand to the side as Sebastian talks to two police officers in uniforms. They arrived within minutes after the fight ended.

Sebastian hauled the guy who had hit him to his feet and handed him over to one of the officers who placed handcuffs on him. By that time, the drunken jerk was sobbing about how sorry he was and that he didn't want his parents to find out what he'd done.

I listened to the bartender explain that she was the one who called 9-1-1 to report that a policeman had been punched in her bar. The squad car came screaming down the street with the siren blaring and lights flashing.

"Just throw him in lockup overnight, Tim." Sebastian pats the back of one of the uniformed officers as the other leads the handcuffed man out of the bar. "He needs to sober up."

"It looks like he got you pretty good." Tim raises his chin. "Do you need to be checked out?"

Sebastian shakes it off with a wave of his hand in the air. "No broken bones. It's just a little blood."

It's more than a little. The blood that trailed onto his shirt also splattered on the lapels of his jacket. He wiped most of the blood from his face with a few paper napkins the bartender handed him.

Tim turns toward the doorway. "You're a better man than me, Detective. I wouldn't let him off so easy."

Sebastian chuckles. "I'm considering sending him my dry cleaning bill."

"I feel like I should take care of that for you." The bartender takes a few steps so she's standing next to Sebastian as Tim leaves. "None of this would have happened if you weren't defending my honor. I'm Chelsie by the way."

Sebastian's gaze skims her face. She's cute. Her hair is red, her body curvy. She's definitely the same type physically as Wendy.

"It's my job to step in if I notice a disturbance." He swipes another napkin under his nose. "You should think about security if this is a regular occurrence."

"I'm just about to close up for the night." She looks around the bar. A lot of the patrons cleared out after the fight, but there are still a few people lingering. "You can stay for a beer. Consider it a thank-you. We'll talk about those extra security measures."

Seriously? Is she hitting on him right now?

He looks past her shoulder to lock eyes with me. "I have plans."

"You can't break them?" She steps closer to him. "The beer would be on the house and I live upstairs. You can get cleaned up before I thank you for what you did tonight."

He smiles at me. "I can't break them. I'm going home with the beautiful woman I live with."

She steals a glance over her shoulder at me. "I'm sorry. I didn't realize you were with someone. My mistake."

"No harm, no foul." He strums his fingers on the top of the bar before he walks past her, reaching out to me. "Let's get the hell out of here."

I place my hand in his. "I'm all for that."

***

The looks Sebastian got on the subway weren't shocking to me. New York City is filled with one unexpected visual surprise after another, but a tall, handsome man in a suit covered in blood splatter will draw more than a few stunned glances and whispers.

We sat next to each other on the train as Sebastian talked to his lieutenant on the phone about what had happened at the bar.

Judging from what I could hear of Sebastian's side of the call, she had been notified by one of the uniformed officers of the fight. He laughed it off and explained to her that the man who had hit him was drunk.

He assured her that he didn't need to see a doctor and then he told her he'd see her the day after tomorrow.

The entire time he spoke with her he held my trembling hand.

I'm still shaking as we walk into the foyer of our apartment.

"Are you cold?" It's the second time he's asked me that. The first time was on the subway platform when we were waiting for the train. He was ready to slide his suit jacket off to drape over my shoulders, but I'd insisted that I was okay.

"No. I'm fine," I say under my breath as I wait for him to unlock the apartment door.

He motions for me to go first and I do. He flicks on the light switch and the room fills with the warm glow from the chandelier above the dining room table. "What a night."

I look back at him. The skin around his nose is starting to bruise. "Maybe you should use an ice pack on your nose. I keep one in the freezer."

"I saw it the other day." He slides his suit jacket from his body. "It's next to the container of ice cream that expired two years ago."

I know he's trying to make me smile, but it's not going to work. The image of him being hit keeps running on an endless loop in my mind.

"I need to shower." His hands make quick work of the buttons of his dress shirt. "I'll wash the shirt tomorrow and drop off the suit at the dry cleaner."

I look down at the bloodied clothes on the floor. "Why aren't you pressing charges?"

He rubs his jaw. "He meant no harm."

I almost laugh. "He punched you in the face. He meant to harm you."

He maintains eye contact, never wavering. "He's young, Matilda. He was drunk. He's a first-year med student at Columbia with no prior arrests. I'm not going to fuck up that kid's life because he's a lightweight who can't handle a few beers."

"So he gets a free pass?" I hear the indignation in my voice. "It's fine now to punch someone in the face? You can assault a police officer and walk away?"

"I'll drop by his dorm room in a couple of days to remind him to keep his fists to himself." He unbuckles his belt. "If he were a repeat offender, he would be in front of a judge tonight."

Frustration tenses my neck. I reach back to squeeze it, my hand still shaking.

"Let me." He rounds me in an instant, his large hand leaping to my neck. His touch is soft and gentle. "You're still shaking."

I am. I clench my hands together, but it does little to stop the quivering. "It's been a long day."

His hand slows. "Shower with me, Matilda."

My heart hammers inside my chest, a rhythm I've never felt before. I don't turn to look at him. "I don't think that's a …"

"Good idea?" he questions. "Why not?"

Because we had a twenty-second kiss that transported me to a place I've never been before where I felt safe and wanted. It thrilled me and scared me.

"You've seen me naked," he says in a dangerously low tone. "I've seen you practically naked."

I spin on my heel, leaving his hand dangling in the air. "Tonight felt like a lot, Sebastian."

"The kiss or the punch?" His blue eyes sear into me.

"All of it," I admit. "I'm still processing it all."

"I understand," he says in a calm and controlled tone. "Tomorrow our kiss is the only thing I'm going to remember about tonight."

I squeeze my eyes shut, warding off my warring emotions. I want to cry and laugh, scream and hurl something at the wall out of anger. I hate that someone hurt him and love that he can see so much potential in others, even if they don't deserve it.

"I'll be in the shower." He unzips his pants. "The invitation to join me is still on the table. It will help you relax and you have my word that we won't do anything you're not ready for. You set the pace. I follow your lead."

I nod as I rub my chin. "I'll wait here."

"I understand." He leans forward to sweep his lips over my forehead. "I'll be back in a few minutes."

I stand in silence as he walks toward the main bathroom, leaving me wondering if I should throw caution to the wind and follow him.

Chapter 30

Sebastian

I let the warm water run over my face. It hurts like hell. I checked out my reflection in the mirror before I stepped into the shower. My nose is already swollen; light bruising shadows the skin in the center of my face.

Luckily, I have a scheduled day off tomorrow. By the time I walk into the squad room again, I'll be mostly healed.

Listening to the people I work with chiding me over taking a punch to the face isn't on my bucket list.

I turn so the water hits my back, sharp needles of warmth that take the edge off.

I open my eyes when I hear the groan of the hinges on the bathroom door.

"Sebastian?" Matilda's voice calls through the steam. "I'm here."

My cock stiffens instantly, curving up toward my navel. I grab the base, squeezing it hard. I almost moan.

"Come in," I say hoarsely, my voice lost somewhere in my throat as I think about the sight of her nude body.

Christ. I've dreamed about this. I've fucking fantasized about this night-after-night. I've blown my load too many times to count while thinking about touching her.

The glass shower door opens, and she's there.

My hand reaches out to her and she takes it.

I rake her over as she steps closer to me.

Her tits are round perfection with pink nipples that are already hardened into tight points.

Her skin is flawless. I drink in every inch of her stomach and her toned legs that lead up to her waxed mound.

"Matilda," I whisper her name against her lips as I kiss her. "You're beautiful."

Her hands reach for my biceps. "I've never done this before."

"You've never showered with a man before?"

Her head shakes in silence.

I turn her around, not wanting to touch her skin with my cock because I swear to fucking hell I am one second away from coming all over her.

"I'll wash you," I whisper into her ear from behind. "If it's too much, you tell me to stop."

She nods, her body relaxing slightly at my touch.

I soap my hands before I trail my fingers over her neck, pushing her hair to the side. She shivers slightly, her body shaking.

I look down and the sight of her ass almost drops me in place.

It's just as I remember when I saw her in her lingerie, but now it's bare, tempting me to touch it and kiss it.

"I was scared at the bar," she admits with a sigh.

I trace the curve of her back with my fingertips. "I know."

I could see it in her face when I looked for her after taking the guy to the ground. She was staring at me, her expression a mix of confusion and fear.

I would have run to her then and taken her in my arms, but I couldn't.

Instead, I smiled, hoping that it would offer her some reassurance that I was all right.

It didn't. Her bottom lip had trembled, but she'd stilled it with her teeth when she bit into it.

My hand moves lower and she adjusts her feet, spreading her stance. I take it as a silent invitation and glide my fingers lower until they skim the cheek of her ass.

That turns her around. "Sebastian."

I tilt her chin up with my fingers until our eyes meet. "You tell me what you want. I'll never push for more."

"What happens when it's over?"

The words spear me. I've never thought beyond the fuck with any woman before, yet the idea of ending this, even before it's started is twisting my gut.

"I don't know." My voice is so soft I doubt she can hear me.

"We don't have to think about it tonight," she says as she rises to her tiptoes to press a kiss to my mouth. "Tonight I just want to feel, not think."

"You're sure?" I ask because I won't take unless she's certain.

"My bed or yours?" she whispers.

I take her face in my hands and kiss her hard, pushing her lips apart so I can taste her breath. "Mine. I want to fuck you in my bed."

***

We made it as far as the hallway before I pinned her against the wall, wrapped her wet legs around me and kissed her again.

I want to slide my dick into her warmth but I won't without a condom.

Instead, I've got a hand under her, my fingers trailing over her slick flesh, circling her clit to chase her toward the edge.

She bucks against my touch. "God, this is too much, Sebastian."

It's not nearly enough. I haven't tasted her yet. My dick hasn't slid between her plump lips and down her throat.

I want to be inside her, pumping my cock into her while I watch her come undone for me.

I slide two thick fingers inside of her and she grips me. It's so tight that my cock throbs with need.

"Come," I bite out. "Come so I can fuck you."

Her fingernails dig into my shoulders when she flies over the edge into a heated orgasm. Her pussy trembles around my fingers as I press her harder to the wall to keep my knees from buckling. I watch every move she makes, drinking in the sight of her and the sounds she makes as she climaxes just for me.

Chapter 31

Tilly

"When's the last time you were fucked?"

I look down to where his cheek is resting on my thigh.

He's been teasing me with the tip of his tongue since he brought me into his bedroom. He put me on the bed, crawled over me and settled between my legs.

"I know the last time you fucked." I throw my arm over my face. "Wendy, right? Or was it more recently than that?"

"Matilda." His voice comes out as a low warning. "Don't."

I smile to myself as I feel his tongue whip across my swollen clit again. "Don't ask me questions that you're not willing to answer yourself."

That earns me a brush of his teeth over my tender flesh. I squirm to get more. I need more. I came in the hallway, but he's been torturing me like this for what feels like an hour, although I doubt it's been more than fifteen minutes.

"You're so tight." He licks a finger before he slides it inside of me. "I can't wait to fuck you."

His words send a jolt of need to my core and I clench around him.

"Lick me," I whimper. "Or fuck me."

His tongue lashes my clit. "Patience."

I have none right now. I don't care that he knows it. It's been months since I've been with a man, and he had nothing on Sebastian. Foreplay, to my last lover, was a kiss on my mouth and one sweep of his hand over my panties before he pushed them aside and slid his sheathed dick in.

"I want you." I know it sounds shameless, but I feel more comfortable with him than I've ever felt with a man before.

"You want me to fuck you," he growls. "You want my cock, don't you?"

I nod as I look down at his face.

His nose is swollen and the bruising has darkened, but he's still gorgeous.

He kisses the inside of my thigh softly before he moves to cover my sex with his mouth.

"Oh, please," I whimper as I feel my pulse race. "Just like that."

He moans against my clit as he takes it between his lips to suck.

I buck my hips, wanting to feel more. My hands get lost in his hair and when the heat races through me, I call out his name as I come again under his touch.

***

"Fuck," he hisses the word out from between clenched teeth. "Look at us."

I look down at where the wide crown of his cock is resting against my pussy. He put on a condom after I came. I watched his every move, captivated by his muscular, cut body and that cock that I haven't stopped thinking about.

I saw it the first night we met, but this is different.

Tonight he's all mine.

His hand cradles my ass to tilt me up, angling my body. "Relax, Matilda. I need you to relax."

I nod as my eyelids flutter shut under the weight of my desire. "Please, just fuck me."

He chuckles and it rumbles through his chest and into mine. We're pressed so tightly together.

Forehead-touching-forehead.

Body-against-body.

Heart-to-heart.

"Don't rush me." He presses a kiss to my neck, his breath trailing over my flesh. "I want this to last all night."

I want that too.

He slides into me with one delicious long stroke and I tremble beneath him.

"This is incredible," he says in a ragged breath. "I've never felt…"

My breathing drowns out his words as I writhe beneath him when he pumps into me in deep, measured strokes.

I whimper and moan through each thrust, whispering words that I don't recognize, sounds I've never heard myself make.

His lips find mine in a frenzied, fevered kiss that pushes me into the throes of another orgasm.

I come hard around him, screaming his name against his mouth before he flips me on my side, pushes my leg up and fucks me hard.

He groans my name when he comes. His cock is hard and thick as he thrusts deep in furious strokes before he collapses next to me.

Chapter 32

Tilly

I roll over onto my side and immediately I'm flooded with confusion. I sit up in the bed. I'm nude in my bed.

I know for a fact that I didn't fall asleep here. I did that in Sebastian's bed in his arms after we made love.

He was telling me about his first day on the job as a police officer when his deep voice lulled me to sleep.

It's morning now.

The sun is pouring in through my windows. My blinds are open. The spot next to me is still smooth and the blanket untouched.

He must have carried me in here at some point.

I was in his bed last night, wasn't I?

I didn't dream what happened. I couldn't have.

I dip my fingers between my legs and wince at the spark of pain when I touch my pussy. It's swollen and tender.

We were together and now we're not.

I stand and cross the room to my closet. I tug my short blue silk robe from a hanger and wrap it around me.

The chill in the air bites at my skin as I open the door of my bedroom and peer out. I don't see or hear anything.

I tread quietly across the apartment to the hallway.

I stand in place staring at the door to Sebastian's room. It's ajar.

"Matilda?" His deep voice startles me enough that I jump.

I spin around to face him.

It's obvious that he's showered and shaved. He's dressed in jeans and a blue button-down shirt. The bruising around his nose hasn't faded at all, but some of the swelling is gone.

"You're dressed." I point out the obvious as I tug on the sash of my robe to tighten it. "How did I end up back in my bed?"

His gaze darts to the open door of my bedroom. "I had a nosebleed early this morning. I wanted to get my sheets into the wash, so I carried you to your bed and tucked you in."

That makes sense.

I notice the keys in his hand. Maya had a washer and dryer installed in the closet at the end of the hallway when she moved in. He didn't have to leave our place to do his laundry.

"Did you go out?"

He looks down at the keys. "I had to meet someone earlier."

Someone? That's vague enough to pique my interest.

I know he has the day off, but I ask because my curiosity is pushing me to. "Was it a work thing?"

His eyes narrow as he weighs his response. "No work talk today. We both have the day off."

Anxiety bites at me as I weigh his answer. I know his work is shrouded in mystery. It's not like he can tell me about the cases he's working on. I get that his job doesn't fit into the typical nine-to-five box.

"I should shower too." I change the subject. "When I'm done, we can go to my favorite breakfast place if you're hungry."

"Or I can have another taste of you." He closes the space between us with a few wide strides. "Let me eat you before you shower, Matilda."

I don't protest when he pulls on the sash of my robe to loosen it. I only moan in response when he lifts me up and places me down on the sofa. As he kneels on the floor and slides his tongue between my legs, I let the world disappear one more time.

***

"Let's talk about Maya and Julian." Sebastian chews on the corner of a piece of toast.

I look around the interior of Crispy Biscuit, my favorite diner. I've been coming here for the past year. I discovered it by accident one day when I was looking for a sandwich shop I was supposed to meet a blind date at.

My date was waiting for me a block over.

I canceled on him, ordered the lunch special and sat at the counter talking to the owner, Jo. She's one of the friendliest people I've met in Manhattan and whenever I get a chance, I stop in for the food and her company.

"Let's not." I sigh.

"Why not?" he questions as he swallows a mouthful of coffee.

I knew this conversation was on the not-too-distant horizon, but I had no idea we would be diving into it while I'm enjoying Eggs Benedict.

I set my fork down and look at him.

His hair is still mussed from when I tugged on it while I came against his face. I almost drifted off to sleep again after that, but the ring of his cell phone pushed me back into reality.

He didn't answer it. Instead, he got to his feet, leaned down to kiss my left breast and then helped me stand.

I took a shower, got dressed in jeans and a blue sweater and braided my hair. When I walked back into the main living area, he was waiting for me on the sofa staring at the windows. He was lost in thought and when I finally cleared my throat, he turned to find me standing next to him.

I didn't ask what he was thinking about. I can't begin to imagine the weight of his world.

"Maya was trying to set me up with you for months." I push my plate aside. "I kept telling her I wasn't interested."

"I know." He skims his tongue over his bottom lip. "Julian told me as much. I took it to mean you weren't interested in getting involved with a good friend of his. I admit I was hesitant too."

I let out an exaggerated sigh. "It's an odd dynamic, isn't it? We're both important to them. We slept together. When it ends, we are still going to end up running into one another whenever they have a family gathering."

He stares at me, his jaw ticking. "I think we're both mature enough that we can handle it, Matilda."

My heart dips. I'm trying to be mature, but it's not working.

The sex was phenomenal.

I like being around him. I love talking to him. I'm crushing like mad on this man and I don't know what it's going to feel like in the future when I see him with another woman.

I fist my hands in my lap. I can't let my heart race circles around my common sense anymore.

I've done that in the past and it's always ended up with me being dumped because I've gotten too attached.

I want to enjoy this for as long as it lasts, not derail it because I want more than he can give to me.

"I can handle it," I half-lie.

"Good," he responds quickly. "That's settled, so there's nothing to worry about."

Chapter 33

Sebastian

There's nothing to worry about?

Famous last words.

The level of bullshit pouring out of my mouth this morning must be directly related to the punch I took last night.

I'm not a liar yet I'm sitting in this diner telling a woman I'm falling head over heels for that I'm going to be fine when this ends.

My intention when I started the conversation was to discuss how we would tell Maya and Julian that we are seeing each other.

It drifted into something else at Matilda's beckoning. She made it clear that she sees an expiration date for us.

I can't consider that possibility yet because I can still taste her on my lips.

I bow my head in an effort to keep my composure.

"Jo," Matilda calls out. "There you are."

I'd heard her ask for the owner when we first arrived and the woman behind the counter had told her that Jo was out running an errand.

Disappointment washed over Matilda's expression but that quickly morphed into satisfaction when she ordered her breakfast. I insisted she order for me too.

She did. I just polished off a plate of eggs, bacon and hash browns.

"Tilly, it's so good to see you." Jo approaches from the left with her arms outstretched. She slows as she nears our table. "And Detective Wolf?"

Matilda's gaze bounces from my face to Jo's. "You two know each other?"

Jo's hand lands on my shoulder. She gives it a light squeeze. "This one saved my life."

I place my hand over hers as I look up into her face. Her brown hair is tied back into a low ponytail. Her mascara is smeared but her eyes have the same kindness that's always been there.

"You're exaggerating."

She steps away from me so she's closer to Matilda. "When he was a beat cop in the neighborhood, he'd stop in for breakfast. "

"A beat cop?" Matilda's brow furrows.

"I patrolled the neighborhood on foot early in my career." I look out at the sidewalk beyond the windows. "I walked past this place for three weeks before I sat down at that counter."

"I was just about to close down." Jo hangs her head. "Business was bad. I told him as much and the next day he had every cop in the city lined up outside."

I scratch my chin. "Now you really are exaggerating. I asked a few guys from the station to stop by. Word spread and they all had a good meal."

"I got a second chance." Jo sighs. "I was an overnight success because of you."

I nod at the empty plate in front of me. "The food is the key to your success, Jo. You can't keep them coming back unless you're serving what they want."

"I'm grateful for you sending them my way in the first place." She reaches to pick up my plate. "I see that things haven't changed since you made detective."

I narrow my eyes. "What's that supposed to mean?"

"Someone clocked you in the face." Her finger brushes the tip of her nose. "They did a good job. Are you all right?"

I look over at Matilda and the wide grin she flashes. "I've never been better."

Jo's gaze volleys between the two of us. "Friends or more?"

"Both," I answer quickly, not wanting to hear Matilda categorize me as strictly her friend.

"Good." Jo reaches to pick up my coffee mug. "I think I'm looking at a match made in heaven."

"What?" Matilda asks with a nervous tremor in her voice.

"You're an angel." Jo smiles down at Matilda before she looks at me. "You're a hero. You two belong together."

Matilda waits until Jo walks away before she speaks. "I should take off. I promised Kate I'd stop by her shop today to help with a delivery. I'll see you at home later?"

"Sure." I nod. "I'll pick up the check."

"You did last time." She fumbles in her bag for her wallet. "It's my turn. We split all expenses, remember?"

I don't need a reminder of what I said. I want to pay for the meal, and hold her hand as we go to the clinic. I want to take her home and back to my bed for the rest of the day. For all the days, and nights. Maybe forever.

"I'll be home in a couple of hours." She stands and leans toward me, but stops herself.

I watch her walk over to Jo, push a few bills into her hand and then leave without looking back.

Chapter 34

Tilly

"I didn't think you'd show up," Kate says when I arrive at her store. "I've asked you to help me sort through deliveries how many times?"

At least a half dozen since we met.

It's become a running joke between us.

She'll tell me that she's expecting a delivery and could use a hand in exchange for pizza and sodas and I'll tell her that I just ate.

"I'm here because I don't want to be a liar," I blurt out.

Her eyes widen. "You're going to need to explain that. What's going on?"

I close the space between us with a few steps. "I was having breakfast with Sebastian and needed some air. I told him I had to come here to help you."

"Breakfast with Sebastian?" Her hands reach out to grab my shoulders. "Are we talking about a morning after breakfast, Tilly?"

I inch up my brows.

Her gaze darts around the store and the customers who are perusing the dresses. She lowers her voice to a whisper. "Did you two fuck last night?"

"Yes," I say quietly.

She slides one of her hands into mine, tugging me forward. "This way. We're going to my office. I want all the details."

I follow closely behind her as she stops to talk to customers on our way to the back of the store.

Once we're there, she slams the door of her office behind us before she turns to face me. "You're glowing."

I run my hand over my forehead. "I'm overheated. I walked here from Crispy Biscuit."

"That's twenty blocks." She pushes me toward the chair behind her desk. "Sit down before you pass out."

I take a seat in the chair, grateful for the reprieve for my aching muscles.

She settles on the edge of the desk, smoothing the skirt of the pale pink dress she's wearing. "So tell me how it happened."

I'm not about to run through every small detail of last night. It's not just that it will take too long, but I want to cherish those memories as my own. I don't want them to become tarnished with her opinion of them.

They belong to me.

"He invited me to take a shower with him and I did."

Her gaze slides over my face. "Was he good to you? You're not here because he hurt you or upset you, are you?"

The level of compassion in her tone surprises me. I reach for her hand and squeeze it. "He's a good man. He was so good to me."

"So good as in one time or five times?" Her concern gives way to curiosity.

I laugh at her question. She's asking me how many orgasms I had. "Good as in I lost track."

Her hand darts to the middle of her chest. "At least one of us is having great sex."

I'm grateful it's me.

"You said you needed some air, Tilly. Why?"

I rub my neck. I wasn't expecting her to ask me that and I'm not sure I'm prepared to answer. "We went to Crispy Biscuit for breakfast and Jo was there…"

"I love Jo," she interrupts.

I pause to nod before I continue, "I was about to introduce her to Sebastian, but they already met years ago."

"It's that six degrees of separation thing everyone talks about in this city."

I look down at my jeans. "Jo said that we were a perfect match. She actually used the words *match made in heaven*."

"I'm on team Jo on this one." She crosses her legs at the ankles. "I saw how perfect you could be together the day I met him."

I look up. "He's not looking for anything like that, Kate. He doesn't want a girlfriend. His job is his priority."

She slides to her feet. "Did he come right out and tell you that?"

"Yes, " I say quickly. "It was the day that Wendy showed up at my apartment."

"I thought they might be just fuck buddies." She tucks a lock of her hair behind her ear.

"They're not anymore."

"What do you mean?" Confusion knits her brow. "How do you know that?"

I pause. "Last night when we went for a beer he told me that their arrangement is over."

Her gaze wanders over her desk before she focuses on me. "It sounds like you were on a date last night."

I throw my head back into the soft leather of the chair. "You're impossible. We didn't go on a date. We fucked last night, had breakfast together today and I bailed because I already feel things."

"Heart things?" She points at my chest.

I shrug off the question. "Intense things. I want to spend as much time with him as I can. I want to get back into bed with him and stay there."

"So do those things. You're in love with the way he fucks."

"I'm not in love with the way he fucks," I protest weakly, wondering if that's a real thing because if it is, I may be guilty of it.

"You haven't had sex in a long time," she points out. "You just had incredible sex. It's understandable that your feelings are going to be a jumbled mess."

I scrub my hand over my forehead. "They are all jumbled together."

It's an understatement. I haven't been able to think straight since I got into the shower with Sebastian. Jo's words only added another layer to my confusion.

"Don't overthink this, Tilly." Kate crosses her arms over her chest. "Fucking doesn't have to lead to anything. It can just be mind-blowing sex."

"Do you really believe that?" I ask with skepticism.

She lowers her voice and leans closer to me. "I believe that you can fuck Sebastian and not let your heart get tangled up in the middle of it."

"How do I do that?"

"You keep your wits about you." She looks into my eyes. "Never forget that he's not looking for more. A man like that isn't likely to change just because he enjoys the sex."

"I think I can do that," I whisper.

"You can," she assures me. "Don't miss out on the time of your life because you're busy planning the rest of your life in your mind. Live in the moment. You won't regret it."

I hope she's right. I want to be in Sebastian's bed again. I want to taste his lips, feel his body, and listen to him come.

I don't want my heart to get broken.

I pray that I won't fall in love with him.

Chapter 35

Tilly

"How did things go at Kate's shop?" Sebastian asks as I walk into the apartment three hours later.

I didn't expect to hang out at the bridal boutique for most of the afternoon, but I could tell that Kate did need help since the store was filled with soon-to-be brides looking for the perfect dress.

I opened each of the garment bags that had been dropped off and checked each dress off the corresponding list.

By the time I was done, Kate had made a few sales, her new inventory was checked in and I felt like I could face Sebastian without letting my mind wander to the future.

"Everything is taken care of." I toss my purse and keys on the dining room table. "She owes me pizza and beer now."

"Pizza and beer?" He laughs from where he's standing at the windows that overlook midtown Manhattan. "That's a great way to get paid for your hard work."

My gaze catches on the vase of flowers next to him.

The withering red and yellow bouquet he bought the day after he moved in has been replaced with white roses.

They're my favorite.

"You bought flowers again," I point out the obvious as I cross the room to where he's standing.

His brows draw together as he leans against the windowsill. "Flowers make you smile."

My heart reacts to his words, upping its beats.

He looks back out at the city. "My partner is getting married next week. It's a last minute thing since he's moving to Chicago soon."

"Your partner is leaving?" I look out the window too at the late afternoon sun reflecting off the windows of the building across the street. "So you'll be getting a new partner?"

"That's how it works." His jaw flexes. "The ceremony and dinner will be at a restaurant uptown. I was wondering if you'd like to go with me?"

Now, that does sound like a date.

"I thought it would be good practice for us before Julian and Maya's big day," he clarifies. "We'll check out the maid-of-honor and best man's moves, so we don't mess up when it's our turn to step up to the plate."

This is sounding less like a date and more like a research project.

I nod. "Sure. I'm on board for that."

He kisses my forehead. His lips trail a soft path down to my cheek. "Last night was incredible, Matilda."

I lean back to look into his stormy blue eyes. I see a heady combination of lust and need.

Kate's words circle through my thoughts. I do want more experiences with him. I want to enjoy every second we have together.

I can sleep with this man and keep my heart from diving into a free-fall.

"It was one of the best nights of my life," I whisper as my gaze drops to his lips.

"Let's make tonight the best night of your life." He moves quickly, pulling me into his arms. "I need to go see my lieutenant, but I'll be back to cook dinner and then..."

His words get lost in our kiss. It's slow, sensual, and a promise of what's waiting for me in his bed tonight.

***

"Ah, Christ." He leans back on his bed, his hands fisting the sheets, sweat peppering his forehead. "How, Matilda? How the fuck did you learn how to do that?"

He doesn't want to know that so I don't answer.

I hollow my cheeks again and slide his beautiful, big cock into my mouth.

We've been in his bed for more than an hour.

He made a simple salad for dinner before he tugged me up from my chair, slid my dress off of me and carried me into his bedroom. I was wearing only my white lace bra and panties.

I'm still wearing those, but he's long since stripped himself of his clothes.

He's gloriously naked now, laid out like a feast just for me and I've been taking full advantage of it.

We kissed for what felt like a full thirty minutes while I stroked his dick with my hand, inching him closer to an orgasm.

When he breathlessly announced that he was on the brink of shooting his load all over me, I slid down and took him in my mouth.

He came.

I swallowed every last drop and when he tried to push me down to take care of me, I resisted.

I whispered that I wanted more and he groaned before falling back onto the bed, his cock already hard again.

"Your cock is perfect." I run my tongue over the shaft. Trailing kisses down one side before I leisurely lick the base.

"You love sucking it," he growls. "My cock. You love sucking my cock."

I nod as I inch the tip between my lips again.

"I want to come inside of you." He tugs on my hair to pull my head up. "I need to fuck you."

I'm in control.

My desire matches his demands. I'm going to take him to the edge again with my mouth before I sheath his cock and mount him.

"It's never been this good," he whispers the words into the air.

My hand dips between my legs, wanting to get myself off.

I want to be his best. I want to be the one that he'll never forget.

He stills. "Don't touch yourself. Please. I want that."

His words are breathless and filled with heavy need.

I move quickly, grabbing the condom package he threw on the bed earlier. I rip it open, carefully cover him and slip out of my panties before I lower myself onto his thick cock in one slow, painfully perfect movement.

Chapter 36

Sebastian

It's been three days since I fucked Matilda.

I've never had a night like that. She took me in her mouth with an eagerness I haven't experienced with a woman before.

Many women have sucked me off, but not one of them took their time to savor me the way Matilda did.

She expertly read my body's cues, sucking harder when I needed it before pulling back to lick me softly. She moaned through it all. Those small noises of pleasure made me harder, more frantic to come.

I came the instant I was in her mouth after she stroked my cock while kissing me. That didn't stop her. She was on me again. My cock gliding between her soft lips before she slid her tight pussy over me and rode me hard.

I crave her every second of every day, but our schedules haven't meshed since that night.

She's been working a later shift at the clinic. I've been focused on a new case.

Our interactions have been limited to a brief kiss in the hallway as she leaves the apartment just as I'm getting in.

I crashed at home for three hours late this afternoon after working all night. I crawled into her bed after she'd left so I could fall asleep surrounded by the smell of her.

"Sebastian," Darrell calls from across the squad room. "I thought we were meeting for a drink last night."

Shit. I forgot to text him to cancel.

I rest my hand on my forehead as he nears my desk. "So you came all the way down here to find out why I stood you up?"

He chuckles. "I know why. You'll have an arrest warrant for your suspect in your hand within the hour."

"Good." I lean back in my chair. "That still doesn't explain what you're doing here."

"I'm here to see Brant." He looks around the squad room. "Where is he?"

I shrug. "I have no fucking clue. He's probably out sampling wedding cakes."

Brant's mind hasn't been on the job since he announced that Remy said yes. He's been sloppy and distracted. I've called him out on it twice, but I get it. He's already planning his life in Chicago.

He starts working in narcotics there a week after he leaves New York.

"Speaking of wedding cakes." Darrell drops into Brant's chair. "I got an email invitation to the big event. Do you want to be my plus one?"

"I got one too and I have a date."

"You're bringing a woman to Brant's wedding?" He leans forward on his elbows. "Who?"

I hesitate for a beat before I answer. "Her name is Matilda. She's my roommate."

"That's an upgrade from the guy you were living with."

"I sold my apartment." I look down at the witness statement in front of me. "I rented the extra room in a friend's place. Matilda is her sister."

"So it's a platonic thing?"

"Was," I correct him. "It's more now."

He shoots me an impatient look. "What's the deal with you two? Is it a good time thing or more?"

"It's a one day at a time thing." I feel my shoulders tense. I don't like talking about women with Darrell, or anyone for that matter. I sure as hell don't want to discuss what I'm feeling for Matilda with him.

He pushes back from the desk to stand. "I'm looking forward to meeting this woman at the wedding."

"Don't tell her what an asshole I am at work." I cock a brow. "She thinks I'm a good guy."

He considers my words as he buttons his suit jacket. "She's right. You're one of the good ones, Sebastian."

The jury is still out on whether that's true or not.

***

"Detective Wolf!"

I turn at the sound of a child's voice calling my name. It's Cooper Gallo. He's racing toward me on the sidewalk outside the station with his mother holding tightly to his hand.

"Is this where you work?" He looks up at the building.

"It is." I brush my hand across his forehead to push his bangs from his eyes. "It's good to see you, Cooper. You too, Carolyn."

"Sebastian," she says my name through a deep breath as she adjusts some shopping bags in her free hand. "Cooper spotted you on the other side of the street. We practically sprinted the entire way."

I laugh. "I'm glad you caught me."

"We're going for ice cream." Cooper bounces on his toes. "Can you come with us?"

"Cooper." Carolyn bends so she can look at him eye-to-eye. "Detective Wolf is a very busy man. He's working right now, sweetheart."

I was on my way to grab something for dinner, but I look down at the little boy's hopeful expression. It can't hurt to indulge in ice cream. Besides, Carolyn is a friend to Matilda and she looks like she could use an extra set of hands to help out right now.

I reach to take the bags from her. "I've got some time and I'm craving a scoop of mint chocolate chip."

Cooper drops his mom's hand to take mine. "Do you like the ice cream at Cremza? It's our favorite place."

"Mine too. Lead the way," I reply, wishing I had Matilda by my side.

Chapter 37

Tilly

Now I get it.

I couldn't figure out why the hell Carolyn insisted I leave work to take my dinner break at an ice cream shop with her and Cooper.

I tried to explain on the phone that I was dead tired and eating my sandwich was taking all the effort I could muster, but she was adamant that I leave the clinic to come to Cremza.

I'm glad I did.

Sebastian is sitting next to Cooper and Carolyn.

I don't care that my hair is falling from the messy bun I tied it up in earlier. It doesn't matter that I didn't bother with any makeup but a light coat of mascara today.

I'm wearing scrubs and flat white shoes, but the way Sebastian is looking at me is making me feel like I'm the most beautiful woman in the world.

He stands as I approach.

"Matilda." His voice is rough. "I didn't expect to see you here."

"I didn't expect to see you either." My gaze turns to Carolyn. "In your text you said you had something you wanted to talk to me about."

"I did?" Carolyn blinks at me. "I can't remember what it is right now."

"Hi, Tilly." Cooper tugs on the leg of my scrubs, smearing blue ice cream over the fabric. "We saw where Detective Wolf works."

"I ran into them outside my station." He gestures to an empty chair next to him. "Cooper invited me for ice cream and his smile is too hard to resist."

Cooper flashes us both a toothy grin.

Sebastian waits to sit until I'm settled in the wooden chair. "Do you want some ice cream, Matilda?"

"I'm good," I murmur. "I just ate dinner."

"Dinner," Carolyn repeats the word loudly. "Cooper we need to go home and have dinner."

He rolls his eyes as he takes another lick from the soft ice cream. "We had dinner, mom. We had hot dogs right before we saw Detective Wolf."

She tosses him a glance. "That was an after school snack. It's time to go so I can cook a proper dinner for you."

His bottom lip juts out in a pout. "Mom. You said that the hot dogs were dinner. I heard you."

I bite back a laugh. She didn't factor in Cooper's reaction when she came up with this plan to get Sebastian and me in the same place at the same time.

"I'll make those chicken nuggets you love."

He swings his feet, as he remains glued to his chair, even though she's already standing. "That's okay, mom. I'm full."

Carolyn reaches down to scoop several colorful shopping bags into her palm. "We are leaving now, Cooper. Say goodbye to Tilly and Detective Wolf."

He finally gives in and slides to his feet. Ice cream drips from the cone onto his red hoodie. "Goodbye Tilly and Detective Wolf. I have to go eat chicken nuggets I don't want."

Sebastian and I laugh in unison as Carolyn tugs her son toward the door leaving me alone with the man I've missed more than I realized.

***

"Mint chocolate chip," I whisper as I break our kiss. "That's what you had, isn't it?"

He nods. "Tell me you can ditch work and go home to bed with me."

My body aches at the dark promise in his tone. His hands were on me the minute we saw Carolyn and Cooper leave the ice cream shop.

He scooped my face into his hands and kissed me. It was tender at first, then more demanding. He took my breath away with just the touch of his lips against mine.

"I can't, Sebastian." I rest my forehead against his. "I have to work for a few more hours."

"Me too." He kisses me again, this time with a lash of his tongue over my bottom lip. "I slept in your bed earlier."

The admission draws me closer to him. I edge forward in my seat. My gaze drops to his lap and the noticeable bulge in his black pants. "Did you touch yourself?"

That pushes him back far enough that he can stare into my eyes. "I should have. Shit, I could have with your smell all around me."

I lean forward, sweeping my breath over his ear as I whisper to him. "I did it in your bed last night. I came on your sheets thinking about how it feels when you fuck me."

His lips crash into mine for a wet, heated kiss.

Our tongues collide, our moans get lost in each other's throats and when we part, his eyes bore into me. "I need you. Fuck do I need to be inside of you, Matilda."

"I'll be home at ten." I ease my hands down his broad shoulders. "Be waiting for me in my bed and I promise you'll fall asleep with a smile on your face."

Chapter 38

Sebastian

She meant ten last night, you fucked-up asshole.

I berate myself yet again as I drag myself into our apartment at noon.

It's been hours since I tasted Matilda's lips at the ice cream shop and almost as long since I've heard a word from her.

My current case broke wide open last night after we arrested a man we believed was involved in the murder.

He was ready, willing and incredibly eager to share what he knew because he was scared shitless of his friends who had taken out an innocent bystander in their anger-fueled rampage to get revenge for some guy hitting on one of their girlfriends a week ago.

Once we had the names of everyone involved, we set out to track them down. It took all night, but by day's break, we had two confessions and a third ready to talk in exchange for a reduced sentence.

I handed the entire mess over to Darrell before I left the station.

It's his to sort through. I need to sleep.

I toss my keys on the table as I look toward the open door of Matilda's bedroom.

I know she's not here.

When I sent her a text message last night to tell her that I wouldn't be joining her in bed, she replied that she understood.

She also said she would be meeting her sister for brunch to go over some preliminary wedding plans.

I curse under my breath as I survey the empty apartment.

The silence is deafening. The vase of pink roses sitting next to the white ones I bought a few days ago is a surprising sight.

I stalk toward them, my gaze stuck on a small pink envelope on the table near the vase.

I pick it up.

Tilly Baker is written across the front of it in blue ink along with our address.

It's been opened, so I slide my hand in but come up empty.

I push the roses apart, looking for any sign of a card. When I don't find one, I drop the envelope at my feet and gaze at her open bedroom door.

I want to know who the fuck the other flowers are from.

My strides are long and brisk as I cross the apartment. I stop just outside her bedroom.

I don't have the right.

I can get into her bed and fall asleep in her sheets, but I don't have the right to go through her things searching for a card.

I lean both hands against the wall on either side of the doorframe.

I could do this the easy way and take the envelope to the flower shop that's listed on the back of it. I'd flash my badge, tell them I needed to know who sent them and I'd have that name within ten seconds.

It's wrong on so many levels.

I close my eyes against the urge.

The chime of an incoming text message yanks me back to the moment. I look down at my phone.

Hillary*: Where are you?*

Sebastian: *Why? You ok?*

Hillary: *Can I see you?*

Another message comes in before I have a chance to reply that I'm dead tired and headed to bed.

Hillary: *I really need to talk to you. Please.*

We've talked and talked until she's run out of words. I thumb out a quick response.

Sebastian: This afternoon at 4.

I shake my head when I see that she's typing a response.

Hillary: *Can it be sooner?*

I scrub my hand over the back of my neck when I feel tension take hold of me.

Sebastian: *Now at the Roasting Point Café on Broadway and Seventy-Fourth?*

I start the walk toward my room for a quick change of clothes. I already know what her response will be.

Giving up sleep is a sacrifice I have to make.

I made a commitment to her and I'm a man of my word. I won't let her down. I can't.

***

"You're a million miles away again," Matilda says as walks into our apartment.

It's late. The lights are off, darkness took over the city hours ago, but I haven't been able to drag myself from this spot by the window.

I've been here since I got back from meeting Hillary.

We talked about the same thing we always do. It's the one thing that binds us together.

Pain.

"I'm right here," I answer as I look over at her. "I'm sorry I couldn't get here last night."

"It's fine." She flicks on a lamp near the sofa. The soft light is enough to illuminate her beautiful face. "Your work is important."

"You're more important," I say under my breath.

She doesn't hear me, or if she does, she ignores my words. "Have you eaten yet?"

I look back at the lights of the city. "I met someone earlier. I had a coffee and a bagel."

"The same someone you met the other morning? It was a woman, yes?"

"Yes," I answer briskly.

She closes the distance between us with short, sure steps. Her fingers land on one of the pink roses. She stares down at them. "I'm tired. I think I'll call it a night."

I have no right to ask, but I've been staring at that bouquet for hours. "Where did those come from?"

"Boyd."

What the fuck?

"Your ex-boyfriend?" I don't know why the hell I'm asking for clarification.

She scratches the side of her nose. "He's the only Boyd I know."

"Why is he sending you flowers, Matilda?"

Her eyes search mine. "If you want an answer to that, I'll want an answer to who the person is that you've been meeting."

Fair enough.

I fist my hands to quell the need to reach out and grab her. I want to fuck her against this window until she screams my name. I want every person in this city, and one asshole back in San Francisco to know that she's mine.

I want her to *be* mine.

The bastard sent her pink roses. Her favorite is white.

I ask the question again. "Why did he send them?"

"Because he's lonely?" She shrugs. "He wants to come out here to visit me. I told him to save his money. I'm not interested."

She goes on as she leans down to inhale their fragrance, "I almost tossed the flowers in the trash when they were delivered this morning."

"Why didn't you?"

She glances at me before her gaze falls on the pink roses. "It's not their fault Boyd is a jerk."

I huff out a laugh. "I'm not fucking the woman I met earlier, Matilda. I'm not fucking anyone but you."

She looks to me, holding my gaze as her lips twitch with a smile. "That's all I wanted to know."

She wears jealousy like a badge and I just got a flash of it.

I fucking loved it.

Chapter 39

Tilly

"Dance with me, Matilda."

"You want to dance with me now?" I tug the hem of the T-shirt I'm wearing down.

After Sebastian and I talked about the flowers, I went to shower. He said he was going to do the same. I expected him to ask me to join him in the main bathroom, but he didn't.

I took my time under the warm running water, relishing in the feeling of the calm that washed over me.

When I was done I towel dried my hair, smoothed lotion over my skin and slid on a new pair of red lace panties and this T-shirt.

It's the same T-shirt I was wearing the night we met.

His hand skims the waistband of his pajama bottoms.

I can see the outline of his erection from where I'm standing near the hallway that leads back to my bedroom.

"On the floor." He looks down as he reaches out a hand to me. "I'm not dancing on the table."

Soft music is filling the room. It's coming from the mini speaker I left on the kitchen counter the other night. He must have synced his phone to it.

I take his hand as I near him. "Is this what you were listening to the night we met?"

He nods when he scoops me into his strong arms. "It's relaxing. It soothes me."

He needs that. I see the pain that lives just behind his eyes. It's always there, even if he thinks he can mask it with a smile.

One of his hands slides down to the small of my back. The other grabs hold of my hand to hold it next to his chest.

He smells incredible. Soap mixed with the unique scent that is only his.

I could wrap myself in that forever.

Forever.

I shake my head to chase the thought away.

We sway back and forth to the music, neither of us saying anything.

He finally clears his throat when the song stops and another begins. "I was shot years ago."

I stop in place and look up. "What?"

He reaches up to where my hand is resting on his left shoulder. He slides it down a few inches. "It's a small wound. The bullet entered here and exited through my back."

I squint to have a better look and I see it. There's a circular scar beneath the ink of his tattoo. At first glance you wouldn't notice it, but it's shockingly apparent to me now that I know it's there.

I instantly wonder why Maya never mentioned it to me.

"When did that happen?" I inch my fingers over his skin to touch the scar.

He sucks in a breath. "I was only on the force for a few months at the time."

I wasn't living here then. I was still immersed in my life back in San Francisco. News of the shooting of a police officer clear across the country wouldn't have caught my attention.

That's different now that I know a man who puts his life at risk every single day to protect others; to protect me.

"How?" I inch back, feeling suddenly unsteady on my feet.

"It was a domestic disturbance call." He reaches for both of my hands. "I walked into the middle of a family argument. My partner wasn't out of the car yet before the shots were fired."

"Shots?"

"Two rounds." He squeezes my hands. "The first hit me. Thankfully it was a lucky shot and his aim was shit with the next one. It went straight into the floor."

I hate that he's joking about this.

My heart is hammering inside my chest at the thought of blood gushing from his shoulder.

I could barely handle it the other night when he was punched in the face. I don't know what I would do if he were shot.

"How bad was it?" I ask in a trembling voice.

"If it would have been a few inches lower, it would have ripped through my aorta." He lifts one of my hands to the left side of his chest and presses it against his skin. "I had surgery, went to physical therapy and was out on foot patrol within the month."

I try to find my composure, but my hand is shaking in his. "I'm glad you're okay."

"I told you so you'd know what this was…" He glides both of our hands over the scar. "Before you noticed it or before Julian mentioned it to you."

Of course Julian would know. They've been friends forever.

"My sergeant at the time reprimanded me." He looks at the floor. "I was eager. Way too fucking eager back then. I walked up to the door of that townhouse like I was indestructible."

Sometimes when I look at him, I feel like he is.

"Kiss me, Sebastian."

His lips brush against mine in a soft kiss and I pray that he won't taste the single tear that's running down my cheek.

Chapter 40

Sebastian

I inch her back toward the dining room table as I deepen the kiss. I know I upset her. I fucking told her I'd been shot.

It was years ago, but the pained look on her face transported me back to that day.

I was cocky, inexperienced and unaware of my surroundings. I thought the uniform on my back and the gun at my waist would intimidate anyone enough that they'd step the hell out of my way.

The guy holding a handgun in my direction didn't give a shit that I was a cop.

He just wanted his wife to stay.

She was standing ten feet behind him with a baby girl in her arms and a suitcase at her feet.

I tried to de-escalate the situation, but it was useless.

The bullet ripped through my shoulder and into the wall behind me. I heard another shot before it was over.

He threw the gun on the floor, took a few steps back and dropped to his knees when my partner, at the time, drew his weapon.

His wife shielded their baby in her arms in the corner away from the gunfire.

It was over in seconds, but the impact has lasted for years.

I pull back from the kiss to hold Matilda's face in my hands. "Let me take care of you tonight."

She only nods in response, her eyes searching mine for some reassurance that I'm fine.

The shooting feels like it was a lifetime ago to me, but to her, it's fresh and vivid in her mind's eye.

I slide my hands down to her waist before I pick her up and place her on the table on her ass.

She slithers forward. "Here? Like this?"

I kiss her softly. "Right here."

Her eyes skim my face and body. "You don't have a condom."

"I don't need one." I kiss her cheek before my lips graze a path down her neck. "I'm not fucking you right now. I'm going to use my hand to make you come."

She squirms in place. The red lace panties she's wearing already wet from her need.

I tug her shirt over head and goose bumps crawl up her silky skin.

I lower my mouth to her left breast, plumping it with my hand before I take her nipple between my teeth and bite.

She lets out a yelp. "That hurt."

"You liked it," I say in a low tone. "It felt good."

"So good," she affirms in a moan. "You're so good to me."

I want to be. That's all I fucking want right now is to be everything she needs me to be.

I take her other nipple between my teeth and lash it with the tip of my tongue. Her hand dips to her navel but I still it with my moan.

"It's mine. It's all mine."

The force of my words makes her groan. "Jesus, Sebastian. That's so hot."

I inch my hand lower until it skims the waistband of her panties. I trace a path to the side, bunching the thin fabric in my hand before I tear it apart in one swift movement.

She looks down, her eyes wide saucers of wonder.

"You just…" her voice gets lost in the sound of pleasure that flies out of her when my fingers graze her clit.

I rip the panties away from her body. We both watch the shredded pieces of lace fall to the floor.

I step closer to her, wrapping her legs around me as I slide two fingers into her tight channel.

"Yes," she hisses under her breath.

"Yes," I echo against her mouth.

I finger her slowly. It's a taste of what I'll do to her in my bed before the night is over.

I can't get enough of her.

I'll always want more. That should scare the fuck out of me, but it doesn't.

It offers me a sense of peace I've never felt before.

***

Tears prick at the corners of my eyes.

I'm not crying. If I were, it would be tears of joy.

I'm straining to contain myself because I'm buried in Matilda's pussy and she's clawing the sheets like a wild animal that can't be tamed.

"You like it this deep," I growl as I fold myself over her back.

She's on her stomach. Her beautiful plump ass is resting against me as I drive my dick into her with long, even strokes.

Sweat peppers every inch of my skin and hers.

We've been fucking for hours.

I brought her to orgasm with my fingers on the dining room table. She blew me in return.

Then I licked her while she rode my face on the sofa before I carried her to my bed and slid my dick between her perfect tits.

Now, she's inching her ass closer to my body as I try with every ounce of strength I have left not to come before her.

"Come," I demand, my voice an angry roar.

"Fuck me harder." She screams. "Harder."

I do. I brace my foot on the bed and pound into her with deep, measured thrusts.

I hold her in place with my hands, pinning her to the mattress.

I feel her inch closer, her pussy gripping me like a vise. "I'm going to…"

"Come," I say one last time as she rides my dick to her climax before I lose control and come hard chanting her name.

Chapter 41

Tilly

"Do you think I look okay?" I adjust the neckline of my navy blue lace dress. "I haven't been to many weddings before. I wasn't sure what to wear."

"You look amazing." Sebastian nudges my leg with his as we sit in two of the chairs that have been set up in the corner of a private dining room in a Greek restaurant in midtown.

We're near an archway made of fresh flowers where Samuel and Remy's wedding ceremony will take place.

I rake him over. "You look pretty good too."

He looks hot-as-sin, which is probably because we fucked before we got dressed to come here.

After our marathon night together last week, we both dove headfirst into work again. I also had to fit in time with Maya and Kate.

Frannie needed me too. Our time together was devoted to late night video calls when she showed me all the matching outfits she's created for her daughters and the dresses she's working on for them to wear at Maya's wedding.

When I saw Sebastian exit his bedroom earlier today, he was dressed only in black boxer briefs.

I couldn't resist running across the apartment and throwing myself into his arms.

He picked me up, took me back into his bedroom and fucked me against the window before we showered together in my bathroom.

"I've missed you, Matilda." He reaches to take my hand.

I watch as he rests it on his thigh. "I've missed you too."

"You'll dance with me after dinner, won't you?" His eyes brighten with the question. "Great things happen when we dance."

A blush creeps up my neck. "We can't have sex here."

"Not here." He lowers his voice. "There's an hourly rate hotel a block over where we can."

"You're going to take me to a hotel to fuck me?" I whisper so the bride's parents don't hear us from where they're seated just a few feet away.

"I don't know if I can last until we get home." He kisses my mouth softly.

I pull back to ask a question I'm not sure I want to know the answer to. "Have you taken a woman there before?"

"Tilly Baker?" A man's voice interrupts us before Sebastian can answer.

I look to the side in the direction of the unfamiliar voice. When I see the person standing next to me, I recognize him instantly. "Darrell Carver?"

I jump to my feet to greet him. He tugs me into his arms for a warm embrace.

"What the fuck, Darrell?" Sebastian stands. "What are you doing?"

The bride's parents shoot us all a look.

"Don't tell me you know each other?" I slip from Darrell's arms to stand next to Sebastian.

"We work together, Matilda," Sebastian says evenly.

Work together?

First, he knows Jo and now he's telling me he works with my favorite pet owner from the clinic?

"Matilda?" Darrell repeats my name. "Tilly. Dammit. You're his Matilda."

His Matilda. He thinks I'm Sebastian's Matilda.

"I'm lost." Sebastian wraps his arm around my waist. "How do you two know each other?"

"Tilly and I met years ago." Darrell glances over at me. "She took special care of our dog at the clinic. She even handled watching over him when we were out of town."

"I was their pet sitter." I look over his shoulder. "Where's Sharon? I'd love to say hi to her."

Sebastian's hand squeezes my waist as Darrell's face drops. "We split, Tilly. It wasn't working anymore."

"I'm sorry. I didn't know."

The thumb of his right hand brushes over his ring finger. "It's been for the best. Sharon's already involved with someone else."

The world can shift in an instant and the Carvers are proof of that. They brought their cocker spaniel in for his yearly check-up just over a year ago.

"I'm going to go over to say hello to Brant, " Darrell says before he walks away.

"I can't believe you two know each other." Sebastian chuckles. "I don't know how the hell we circled each other for so long without actually meeting."

I look up and into his warm blue eyes. "Fate must have known we weren't ready for each other until the night I walked in and saw you in all your naked glory."

He leans in to kiss me but nips my bottom lip between his teeth instead. "You've made me hard, Matilda and in answer to your question…no, I've never fucked a woman at the hotel around the corner."

"Good," I whisper against his lips. "You won't fuck me there either. I'm going to make you wait until we're in my bed."

"You're torturing me." He pulls me closer to him so I can feel his steely erection.

I almost groan aloud, but he catches it with his mouth when he kisses me again.

"I'm not complaining." He straightens when he sees the bride enter the room dressed in a short white dress.

I lean into him as we take our seats.

We sit in silence holding hands as we watch two people in love take their vows.

I can't help but wonder what it would be like to stand next to Sebastian under an archway made of flowers and hear him pledge himself to me for eternity.

I'll never know and that has to be enough for me.

It just has to be.

Chapter 42

Tilly

I look over to where Sebastian is sitting with a few of the detectives he works with, including the groom.

They gathered together after dinner to share stories about Samuel Brant. They all burst into laughter over and over again.

"I had no idea you were the woman Sebastian told me about last week."

I smile at Darrell. He took the seat next to me after Sebastian vacated it. We've chatted for a few minutes about the weather and his new job as an assistant district attorney.

It makes sense now that he knows Sebastian.

As tempted as I am to ask him what exactly Sebastian said about me last week, I'd much rather hear those words from Sebastian's lips.

"Is he easy to work with?" I laugh.

"Is he easy to live with?" he counters.

I take a small sip of the red wine that was served with dinner. "Very easy to live with."

He purses his lips. "Very hard to work with."

I can't read his expression. "Seriously?"

He picks up the bottle of beer he brought with him when he came to talk to me. He takes a pull. "He takes me to task on a weekly basis. There isn't another detective who does that."

That surprises me. The Sebastian I've come to know is caring and kind. He's considerate of others, but I've never seen him at work, so it's impossible for me to understand what he's like when he's there.

"He knows the law better than most of the assistant district attorneys." He puts the beer bottle down. "He's not afraid to speak his mind."

"That's a good thing, isn't it?" I feel the need to defend Sebastian even though Darrell hasn't said anything other than that he's passionate about his job.

"It's a frustrating thing, Tilly." He glances over to where Sebastian is still sitting. "He takes every case he's assigned to heart. If I can't deliver the outcome he wants, I hear about it."

"Some people would call that a passion for the job." I lean back in the chair I'm sitting in. "I can tell that his job weighs on him. I'm sure he just wants justice for the victims."

Darrell scratches his chin. "You're right, but his talents would be better suited working for the district attorney."

I cock my head. "You think he should be a lawyer?"

"I know he should be a lawyer," he corrects me. "He was accepted to NYU Law School years ago and passed on it."

"I didn't know that."

I'm surprised by his admission. I knew Sebastian had an interest in becoming a lawyer, but I had no idea it had progressed to the point of him applying and being accepted into law school.

"I told him the other day that I had a friend who is connected to the Dean of Admissions at NYU Law. I offered to put in a good word for him."

I furrow my brow. "Are you talking about Ronald Dixon?"

Ronald is another client I met through the clinic. His cat was brought in late one night after being hit by a car. I just happened to be the vet assistant on call. I comforted him in the waiting room while Dr. Hunt performed surgery on its broken leg.

During the procedure, Ronald told me all about his life, including his job at NYU Law School.

"Let me guess?" Darrell chuckles. "He has a pet who is a friend of yours."

I smile. "You know it."

"You should work your magic and convince Sebastian to apply again." He reaches for his beer. "He passed on his dream job to fulfill a duty to his father and grandfather."

"You don't think he wanted to be a police officer?"

His gaze sweeps over Sebastian and the other detectives. "I think he did what he felt he needed to for his family. He put their dreams before his own."

"He wouldn't still be talking about becoming a lawyer if it wasn't in his blood," he goes on as he pushes back from the table. "He's got a brilliant legal mind, Tilly. He'd be a remarkable lawyer."

My chin lifts. "I'm glad we ran into each other today."

"Me too. Can I ask a favor?" he asks with a grin as he stands.

I narrow my eyes. "What would that be?"

"You must know a lot of people in this town. Do you know any intelligent, kind and fun single women who might be interested in getting to know a newly-single assistant district attorney?"

I lift my hand to my chin as I consider his request and then it hits me. "I do know someone. I'll talk to her next week and if she's interested I'll get her to call you."

"You still have my number on file at the clinic, right?"

I nod. "I do."

"I hope I'll hear from her."

He will. Once I tell Carolyn about Darrell, I think she'll realize that waiting around for the man she had dinner with to call for a second date is nothing but a waste of her time.

I may have just found the next match made in heaven.

"Are you smiling like that because of me?" Sebastian asks from where he's now standing next to me. "I'm ready to leave if you are, Matilda."

I look into his eyes. "What about that after dinner dance you promised me?"

He bends down to kiss my forehead. "I have something else in mind that I think you'll like even more."

Chapter 43

Sebastian

"It's huge, Sebastian."

I smile. "You can't get a better view of it than right here."

She finally backs away from the telescope to look at me. "I had no idea that the moon looked like that. I've only seen it with my naked eye."

Naked.

It's how I want her and she will be soon, but when we got home from Brant's wedding, I wanted to show her the full moon through the lens of my telescope.

"This isn't the telescope that you got when you were a kid, is it?"

I look up at the sky. "That one is long gone. I bought this one for my twenty-fifth birthday."

It was an investment I made in myself. At my old building, I'd spend hours on the roof gazing at the stars. Tonight is the first time I've brought it out here.

It felt right to share that experience with her.

"I get the fascination now." She pushes her hair back when the light wind whips it against the side of her face.

She's the most beautiful woman I've ever known. The most beautiful I'll ever know.

"I can teach you about the stars." I sweep my hand in the air.

She reaches up to fist her hand in her hair. "I'd like that."

"We can go back to the apartment now." I watch her as her eyes take in the night sky.

"Look." Her hand leaves her hair to dart out in front of her. "Isn't that a shooting star?"

I close the distance between us with a few steps as I glance in the direction she's pointing. "It is."

She grabs hold of the lapels of my suit jacket. "We each have to make a wish."

I know the routine. I did it throughout my childhood, but not one of those shooting star wishes ever came true.

"Close your eyes and make your wish." Her lips brush my chin. "Do it now before it's too late."

I do. I close my eyes, rest my head against hers and wish for a lifetime of moments just like this.

When I open my eyes, I catch her wiping a tear from her face.

"What did you wish for, Matilda?" I whisper.

"I can't tell you…"

"Or it won't come true?"

She nods. "I really want this wish to come true."

I run the pad of my thumb over her bottom lip before I kiss her softly. I want to make it come true. I want to make every single one of her wishes a reality because I'm falling in love with her.

***

Her lips part but the only sound that escapes is a moan so quiet I have to still my breath to hear it.

I'm on top of her. My forearms are bracketing her head, my chest pressed against hers as I fuck her slowly.

We're in her bed tonight. She insisted and I didn't argue.

I just wanted to be with her, kiss her and touch her.

"I'll never forget tonight."

I slow the pace of my thrusts even more. "I won't either."

Her hands glide down my back, reaching for something, trying to pull me closer. "I love how you make me feel."

I bury my face in her neck to hide the onslaught of raw emotions I feel.

"Matilda," I say her name against her soft skin. "You're incredible."

Her hips circle as I drive into her again.

"This is what it's like to make love." She heaves out a ragged breath.

I kiss the side of her neck again and again as I stroke my cock deeper with each lunge.

She clenches around me and as she comes, I pull back, cup her face with my hands and stare into her intense blue eyes.

My control shatters at the sight of her. I climax, making a noise so twisted with both pain and pleasure it carries her straight into another orgasm.

Chapter 44

Tilly

"He's your boyfriend." Kate looks over at a group of kids lined up by the zoo's entrance. We're sitting on a bench enjoying the mid-morning sunshine. "You can call him your roommate or your lover or whatever you want, Tilly, but the man is your boyfriend."

Whatever he is, we had an incredible night together.

After we made love, we slept in each other's arms until Sebastian had to leave before dawn.

I got out of my bed and sat on his while I watched him get ready for work.

I soaked in every movement of his body, every word he was saying. I wanted to etch it all into my mind.

I fell back asleep in his bed after he left. When I woke up I showered in his bathroom, using his shampoo and body wash. I was relaxing in my robe when my best friend called to invite me for coffee since it's her day off too. I got ready quickly, choosing a pair of jeans and a red blouse before I straightened my hair and headed out the door.

"Nothing has changed, Kate," I say even though, for me, everything has changed.

I've fallen in love.

I realized it for the first time last night on the roof when we saw the shooting star.

I wished for a lifetime with him.

It brought a tear to my eye and when he kissed me tenderly afterwards, I felt a sense of calmness I've never experienced before.

She turns to look at me. "You're in love with him."

I scrub my hand over my face as if that will wipe away whatever she's seeing. "Why would you say that?"

She runs her fingers through her long hair. "Because it's the truth. It's obvious to me. It must be obvious to him."

I look toward the zoo. It's become one of my favorite spots in Central Park. "It's not obvious to him."

"So you are in love with him?" Her voice is hopeful.

I nod without turning in her direction. "I don't know when it happened, but it did."

"Love is like that." She sighs. "It creeps up on you and before you know it, you're lost to it."

"What am I supposed to do now?" I chuckle. "I fell in love with a man who has made it very clear that he's not looking for love."

"You talk to him." She turns to face me. "You tell him what you're feeling."

"It will change everything between us." My voice trembles. "He'll probably move out."

"Or he might surprise you."

I arch a brow in silent query.

"He might feel the same way about you." She tilts her head. "You have nothing to lose by telling him, Tilly."

"I'll lose what we have now," I point out.

She watches as a woman with a stroller walks past us. "Or you'll lose the chance for more. You won't know how he'll react unless you tell him exactly what you feel."

I look back toward the zoo. "I'll think about it. Are you ready to visit some animals?"

She stands and twirls in place, her long blonde hair flying in the light wind. "How do I look? Do you think they'll like me as much as they like you?"

I laugh as I link arms with her. "They'll love you as much as I do."

***

"Fuck." Sebastian slams his fist into a cushion that's next to him on the sofa. "Goddammit."

I heard him come in when I was on a video call with Frannie. That was ten minutes ago. My sister insisted on telling me all about the wedding dresses she's picked out online for Maya.

I didn't have the heart to tell her that Maya has scheduled another consultation appointment with Kate. When she walked past Katie Rose Bridal the other day she saw the new selection of dresses in the window display.

She believes she'll find the perfect one with the help of my best friend.

"What's wrong?" I ask tentatively from where I'm standing next to my bedroom door. "Did something happen, Sebastian?"

I can tell by his reaction that's he startled. "You're home? I thought you were hanging out with Kate all day."

The bite in his tone sets me back a step. "We hung out earlier. I came home to see if you wanted to get take-out and maybe watch a movie."

"I can't stay." He drops his head back onto the sofa. His knees vibrate under his black dress pants. "I'm sorry. I forgot my wallet this morning so I stopped in to pick it up."

I cross the room with quick steps and settle in next to him. "We'll have dinner another time."

"I wish to fuck I could spend the night with you." His hand lands on my thigh. The sleeves of his white dress shirt are rolled up to his elbows. His muscular forearm tenses as he squeezes my leg. "On days like this I wonder why the hell I joined the force."

"Why did you?" I ask, wondering if he'll confirm what Darrell told me about feeling a sense of duty to his dad.

"To make the city a better place?" He huffs out a strained laugh. "To do the right thing?"

I inch closer until I can rest my head on his shoulder.

He groans audibly when he tugs me into his side. "When I'm here with you the world disappears. I forget all the bullshit, all the pain."

I lean forward to place a soft kiss on his mouth. "I want to take all of your pain away."

He cups my face, his blue eyes searing into mine. "I want that too, Matilda. Fuck, I want that."

Just as his lips brush mine, his cell phone rings.

"Duty calls." He closes his eyes. "I'm sorry. I have to go."

"I know." I kiss him one last time before he scoops his phone into his palm and answers it on his way out the door.

Chapter 45

Tilly

"Again, Tilly." Frannie follows those words with a clap of her hands in front of the camera. "You've been living in dreamland since you left San Francisco. Is it because of Boyd?"

"Boyd?" I lean closer to my phone, so my sister can see the roll of my eyes. "Why would you bring him up?"

"I know he sent you flowers."

"You know?" I sit up straighter on my bed. "How do you know?"

"He called me to ask what color roses are your favorite," she says proudly.

I have no choice but to wipe that smug look off of her face. "My favorite roses are white."

Just like the ones Sebastian bought.

Did he know? Could he have known they were my favorite?

I make a mental note to ask Maya if he asked her.

"No. Our favorite roses are pink," she says matter-of-factly.

I bow my head. I know why she thinks that. Our parents used to send us a dozen roses to share on our birthdays when we were teenagers. They were always pink, Frannie's favorite.

I mentioned to my dad once that I thought white roses were the most beautiful. I was fourteen, and on our fifteenth birthday, another dozen roses were delivered to Frannie and me.

They were pink, all twelve of them.

"I like white roses." I sigh.

Her brows pinch together. "You do? Really?"

She's surprised. Frannie has always felt that we are identical in every way. It's one of the main reasons she took my break-up with Boyd just as hard as I did. She always believed that I'd marry Grant's best friend and we'd live in houses next door to each other, having children who would be not only cousins but best friends.

"You shouldn't have encouraged Boyd to send me the flowers." I rub my forehead. "I'm not interested in him, Fran."

"I saw the way you two were looking at each other when you were here." She bats her eyelashes. "If that's not love, I don't know what is."

What I feel for Sebastian. That's love.

I clear my throat. "I'm never getting back together with him."

"You say that now, Tilly, but…"

I raise my hand to stop her. "Fran. No. It won't happen. Boyd and I will never happen."

She closes her eyes, resting the palms of her hands against them. "I always thought you'd marry him and he'd bring you home."

"Frannie?" I say her name tentatively. "Look at me."

She drops her hands and attempts a weak smile.

"I am home." I push my hair back over my shoulder. "This is my home. I belong here now. I'm building my life here."

"I miss you." She pinches the bridge of her nose.

"I'm a video call away. You can come visit me anytime you want. I'll come back to see you when I get more time off." I smile softly. "But I need to live here."

She nods softly. "I know you're not coming back. I know your life is there now."

I look into her eyes; the eyes that have mirrored mine my entire life. "It doesn't matter where I live, Fran. We'll always be sisters."

"Twins," she corrects me. "Our bond is special."

I watch her closely. Her gaze darts to something to her left before she cracks a wide smile. "Do you need to go make a baby, Fran?"

"How did you know? Grant just walked into our bedroom and he doesn't have a shirt on." A blush creeps over her cheeks.

I smile, wondering if that's what I looked like the first night I saw Sebastian.

"Get the job done." I lean closer to my phone. "I love you."

She presses her lips to the screen of her tablet in a kiss. "I love you too. Find all your happiness there, Tilly. I want that for you."

I want that for me too.

***

"I'm here to see the most beautiful woman in the world." His lips graze over the nape of my neck.

I stretch but don't open my eyes. I can't out of fear that I'm dreaming.

I fought to stay awake until one a.m. hoping that Sebastian would come home. When he didn't, I stripped to my panties, crawled between the sheets of my bed and fell fast asleep.

His strong arms circle me to pull me back and into his bare chest. I can tell that he's nude. His erection is resting against me.

"Unless you're the hottest man on the planet, I'm asleep."

He chuckles and the deep rumble courses through me. "Only you can decide if that's who I am."

"I say it's you and only you," I whisper.

"That makes me the luckiest man who ever walked the face of this earth." He inches even closer.

I take his hand from where it's pressed on my stomach and glide it lower.

"You want to come," he rasps.

I whimper when I feel his fingers brush the lace of my panties. "I want to feel."

He pulls me close, holding my body against his. "You make me feel things I've never felt before."

"What things?" I suck in a deep breath.

"Things like this." He pushes my panties aside to rest the length of his cock between the cheeks of my ass.

I moan. "No condom."

"I know," he hisses. "I won't."

"What other things?" I manage to ask as his finger finds my clit.

His breath runs hot over my neck. "All of this and more."

"More?" I can barely form the word. I'm edging toward an orgasm already. It's all the pent up need I've felt since the last time his hands were on me.

"You know." He glides his finger down. "Move your leg."

His tone is rough, needy. It's filled with raw desire.

I rest my leg over his. My panties are askew, half exposing my pussy. His heavy cock is pinned between us; rigid and thick.

"That's it." He slides a long finger inside of me. "You're going to fuck my fingers. You're going to use me."

"Oh God," I pant, pure need taking over.

I reach down to grab hold of his wrist as I grind myself against his hand while he mouths silent words into the heated skin of my shoulder.

I ride his hand shamelessly, moaning with each thrust, groaning when he slides another finger inside of me, and then another.

"I'm going to come," I whisper in a trembling voice as the orgasm bears down on me.

His lips move from my shoulder. "You're mine. Only mine."

The words push me to the edge. I clench around his fingers as I climax with a loud cry.

He groans, his body shakes and I feel the warmth of his release as it hits my skin.

"Jesus, Matilda." His breath is ragged. "That was incredible."

It was. It was intense and emotional, raw and powerful.

"Sleep," he whispers as he pulls me close again. "Sleep in my arms and dream about me."

"I always dream about you."

"Never stop." There's a tremor in his voice. "And I'll never stop dreaming about you."

Chapter 46

Sebastian

"You can't solve anything by sitting on your ass, partner."

Partner. It's one of the last times I'm going to hear that word coming from Brant. He's packing up his desk. This is his last shift and then he's Chicago bound.

"You'd know that better than anyone, wouldn't you?" I bite back. "You spent more time in that chair the past few months than I've spent in mine the past four years."

"I solved a case or two." He places a framed picture of Remy into a cardboard box. "Homicide isn't in my DNA like it is in yours."

"What's that supposed to mean?" My chin lifts.

"Everyone on the force knows that your grandfather paved the way." He looks over at the lieutenant's office. "He held down this fort. Your dad made it to Detective Third-Grade. You were destined to land in that chair. It's called fate, Sebastian."

My grandfather was at the helm of homicide for more than five years before he took early retirement. The rigors of the job followed him out the door.

He suffered a fatal heart attack right after I joined the academy.

My father's dream of three generations of Wolf men on the force died with my grandfather on a rainy Wednesday evening.

"It's not DNA," I scoff. "It's a commitment to serve the fine people of this city."

He tosses a silver pen into the box. "Finally all the pieces fit together."

I cock a brow. "What pieces?"

"I'm a detective, so I'm trained to observe." His hands drop to his hips. "You've been talking to someone about switching things up. My bet is on a run for City Council after that canned statement you just delivered. Or are you going to sprint right to the finish line and throw your hat into the Mayor's race? I've got to admit I'm surprised you're walking away from all of this."

My head falls back as I laugh. "You've been listening to my phone conversations?"

"Dude, I'm less than ten feet away from you all shift." He opens his desk drawer and pulls out a box of candy bars. "It's not like you're trying to be covert. You knew damn well I could hear you."

"You're an asshole." I wave my hand toward him. "Give me one of those."

He tosses the entire box on my desk. "Consider it a parting gift."

I nod. "I'll put these to good use."

"Liar." He rubs his stomach. "I never took you up on that offer to hit the gym. That's why I'm sporting a belly and you look like an Adonis."

"An Adonis?" I rip open one of the candy bar wrappers and take a bite. "You're creeping me out, Brant."

He holds both hands up. "Remy's sister's words, not mine. She saw you at the wedding. I've been fielding questions about your relationship status ever since."

I don't ask what he told the woman because I don't care.

I have zero interest in anyone other than Matilda.

It's been two days since I've seen her. The last time was when I crawled into her bed and brought her to orgasm with my hand.

The experience was raw and intense. I'm still riding the high of what I felt; what I feel for her.

"I told her you're in love with the woman you brought to the wedding." He places the lid on the box. "Matilda, right?"

"Matilda," I repeat her name back.

He holds up his right hand. "Before you ask how I know that you're in love with her, I didn't hear you confessing that to anyone on the phone. I saw it. In the way you looked at her and in the way she looked at you."

I toss the candy bar wrapper into the trashcan next to my desk. "I'm not going to correct you about how I feel, Sam."

"Good." He pats his hand on the top of the box. "I'm happy for you."

I stand. "You're going to stay safe in Chicago."

"I will." He tucks his hands into the front pockets of his black dress pants. "Where you headed, Sebastian?"

I look around the squad room. It's home. It's been my home for the past four years, but things change. I've changed.

"Not to Chicago," I divert the question since I don't want the entire division to know my plans before my lieutenant does.

He laughs, pushing his hand toward mine. "That's a shame. It's been good working next to you. You're one of the best."

"You'll do good, Brant." I shake his hand. "Take care of yourself."

"You too, Detective Wolf. You too."

I look down when my cell phone chimes.

Alan: ***You got time for a coffee today?***

I glance up to see Brant rounding the corner before he slips out of view. That's another partner gone; another chapter of my life that is over.

Sebastian: ***You doing ok?***

I stare at the screen waiting for his response.

Alan: ***Nah, man. It's been a rough one. Today kicked my ass.***

Sebastian: ***I'll be at diner around the corner from your place in twenty minutes.***

His reply comes through almost immediately.

Alan: ***You're the best. Seriously.***

I slide my phone into the pocket of my suit jacket and head out the door.

I'm not the best. I'm trying to do my best.

I don't know if it's enough.

Chapter 47

Tilly

"I need to take you out for lunch one day this week as a huge thank you, Tilly." Carolyn sits in the chair next to me in the break room.

"It's my job to go over post-operative care with the clients." I push the small fruit salad I brought with me for lunch toward her. "Feel free to indulge. I packed way too much food for myself."

She pops a green grape into her mouth and chews. "I was talking about the set-up with Darrell. He's a great guy."

I gave her his number two days ago. I'm a little surprised that she's called him and gone on a first date within the past forty-eight hours. "I don't know him all that well, but I get a sense that he's one of the good ones."

"He is." She picks up a piece of apple and takes a small bite. "He had a lot of complimentary things to say about both you and Sebastian."

I'm sure that everything positive Darrell said about me was limited to how well I cared for his dog. Sebastian is another story.

It would take one phone call to Julian for me to find out everything I could possibly want to know about the man I'm crazy about. The problem is that Sebastian and I haven't discussed when we'll tell Maya and her fiancé about us, or what we'll tell them about us.

We haven't defined our relationship at all, beyond roommates and friends.

"The last time I saw Darrell we talked about Sebastian too." I shift in my seat.

"Cooper even talks about Sebastian with me. The man has quite the fan club." She laughs as she slides the plastic container of fruit across the table toward me.

I snap the lid back on. "They had a great time together the night we watched Coop."

"Sebastian stopped by here yesterday when you were in with a patient." She eyes the clock on the wall. "He had a solar system book in his hands. He wanted me to give it to Coop. We must have read that thing ten times last night before bed."

I'm both shocked and surprised by the gesture. "I didn't know that."

"He was here to see you." She turns her head to look back at the break room door. "You didn't catch up with him after work?"

I shake my head. "Our schedules haven't matched up this week."

"If I were the one in charge here, I'd give you a day off just to spend with him."

I wring my hands together. "I can't tell you how much I wish you could make that happen."

"You're falling for him, aren't you?"

"I have fallen." I laugh. "I'm gone over the edge and there's no coming back."

"Good." She pushes to her feet. "With any luck, I'll be the next one to fall in love."

***

"I heard that you brought a book to the clinic for Cooper." I rest my head against his right shoulder.

"Office gossip?" Sebastian cocks a dark brow.

I blink. "What do you think?"

His hand cups my cheek. "I think I want to stay in this apartment with you forever. Can you make that happen?"

I nod my chin in the direction of the kitchen. "You'll find a hammer and a package of nails under the sink. Put your big muscles to good use and nail the door shut."

He flexes his left arm under the T-shirt he's wearing. "These muscles?"

"Jesus," I whisper.

His tongue strokes his bottom lip. "I've missed you, Matilda. It's been hell not seeing you for days."

It's been hell for me too.

Every day that we're apart, my heart aches.

I need to tell this man how I feel, but there's still this nagging voice in the back of my head telling me that I'll scare him away if I bring up the *L* word.

Love.

I need to do it soon though. My heart is about to burst open.

"I have a day off on Thursday." My gaze holds his. "Tell me that you do too."

He brushes a strand of my hair back from my cheek before he kisses me softly. "I do, Matilda, but…"

"But?" I almost scream that I don't care what it is. I want this man to myself for more than an hour or two at a time. I want to have a chance to tell him that I'm in love with him without him rushing out the door.

"I have somewhere I need to be."

Somewhere that isn't with me.

"Where?" I ask because I'm on the cusp of begging him to spend Thursday with me.

He closes his eyes and rubs his forehead. "Trust me when I tell you that if I could cancel it, I would, but I can't. It's been in the works for months."

"Is it work related?" I press as I tug on the hem of my white T-shirt.

"It's related to my future." The pad of his thumb skims over my bottom lip. "You've helped me see that anything is possible."

I love knowing that and I want it to be true.

I want to believe that anything is possible.

"Can you give me one more hint about where you'll be on Thursday?" I nip his thumb between my teeth.

He pulls it back and sucks on it. "I'll give you a hint of where I'll be in two minutes."

I laugh. "You'll be right here beside me."

He moves fast. He grabs my waist, picks me up and tosses me on my back on the sofa before he lowers himself to his knees on the floor.

His breath travels hot over my inner thigh before he kisses the outside of my panties. "I'll be tasting this in two minutes, Matilda. Tasting my heaven."

I close my eyes when I feel him slide my panties down and when his tongue lashes at my tender flesh, I get lost in my desire.

Everything else slips away.

Chapter 48

Tilly

"This is for me?"

Bending over, Sebastian kisses me lightly. "This is all for you."

I look down at the wooden tray he placed in front of me when he came walking into his bedroom.

There's a glass of orange juice, one piece of toast and scrambled eggs.

I'm ravenous.

We had the most amazing night. We made love on the sofa and then showered together. Before we went to bed, we took a quick visit to the roof to gaze at the stars.

He sits on the bed next to me. He's already dressed in a navy blue suit and a blue dress shirt.

I have no idea what time it is, but judging by how dark it is outside still, I doubt that dawn has broken.

"Tell me what you do at work, Matilda." He picks up the glass of juice and takes a small sip. "Sometimes in the middle of my day, I stop to imagine what you're doing right at that minute."

I touch the edge of the toast, my hand suddenly trembling. "No two days are ever alike. I suppose, in that way, my job is like your job."

His hand grazes my chin. "Do you know how many times I've walked past Premier Pet Care in the past few years?"

"Once or twice?" I take a small bite of toast.

"Dozens." He gazes into my eyes. "Maybe even more. I had no idea you were right inside."

"When did Maya first tell you she had a sister?"

His mouth curves. "Julian told me. He told me that she had twin sisters. I wanted an introduction right away."

"You did?" That surprises me. Maya had mentioned Sebastian and Griffin, Julian's other close friend, early on in their relationship but I was focused on the men I was matched with on my dating apps.

Once I heard that Sebastian was a police officer, I told Maya I wasn't interested. It was my track record with members of the NYPD that pushed me to decide not to go on a blind date with Sebastian. Now, I'm regretting it because I wasted so much time that I could have spent with him.

"I knew that Maya was an incredible woman, so it made sense to me that you would be too."

"Maya adores you." I take a bite of eggs. "She talked about you non-stop before we met."

"What did she tell you?" He wipes his finger over the corner of my mouth.

"That you were kind and funny."

"Kind and funny?" he balks with a grin. "No wonder you didn't want to hookup with me. She made me sound like I'm boring as hell."

"She made you sound incredible." I caress my hand over his cheek. "You are incredible."

"You'll never stop thinking that, will you?"

How could I? I'll never meet another man like him. I'll never love anyone the same way I love him.

"Never."

"The best decision I've ever made was moving into this bedroom." He pats the blanket. "My life changed that day."

"Mine too." I push my hair back from my cheek.

His gaze darts to the clock on his bedside table. "I have a meeting before work."

I look back at the time. "It's six."

"I'm sorry I woke you." His chin dips. "I've imagined what it would be like to make you breakfast in bed and today I had the urge. You can go back to sleep until it's time for you to go to work."

"Who are you meeting so early?" I breathe. "Most of the city is still asleep."

I see the hesitation in his eyes. It's so apparent that I'm tempted to tell him to forget it, but I don't. I wait in silence for an answer to my question.

"My lieutenant," he answers succinctly. "I need to go over a few things with her, so we're meeting at a diner for breakfast."

"I wish you could stay here with me." I inch the sheet that's been covering me down to expose my breasts.

His gaze follows the path of the sheet. "I wish I could too. You make it hard for me to leave."

I lean forward to brush my lips against his. "One day will you tell me all your secrets, Sebastian?"

The question catches his breath. He stills with his lips hovering over mine. "Only if you promise they won't chase you away."

"I promise," I whisper into the air between us before he presses his lips to mine for a slow, sweet kiss.

Chapter 49

Sebastian

"You picked a hell of a time to fall in love." Liam lowers himself into one of the armchairs in his living room.

My brother lives on the Lower East Side in a one bedroom with a view of the East River. It's decorated with large pieces of leather furniture and reclaimed wood tables.

All of the artwork on the walls is personal to him.

There's a framed drawing that our niece, Winter, did for his birthday. It's nothing more than little scribbles from some brightly colored crayons. To Liam, it's a masterpiece.

A series of photographs line the hallway to his bedroom and bathroom. Those are of our family. Of all my siblings, Liam is the most sentimental; his heart is the softest.

"What's that supposed to mean?" I bite back with a scowl.

"You've got a lot going on right now, Sebastian." He leans forward to rest his forearms on his jean-covered thighs. "You just sold your place. Your partner quit and two of your best friends are getting married."

I set my phone down on his coffee table. "What does any of that have to do with what I'm feeling for Matilda?"

He purses his lips. "It's not uncommon for people to look for an anchor when their life is turbulent."

"You think I'm using Matilda to find some sense of stability in my life?"

He holds up a hand to stop me from saying more. "I've known you for twenty-eight-years. This is the first time I've ever heard you express more than a passing interest in a woman."

"This is the first time I've ever met anyone like her, Wolf."

He pauses for a beat. "I want this for you. It seems fast, Sebastian. You haven't known her that long."

"It's long enough to know she's the one for me." I close my eyes. "She's always with me. I feel her with me now. There's a feeling of peace inside of me that's never been there before. I would lay down my life for this woman."

"Does she feel the same way about you?" His tone softens.

I huff out a laugh. "I sure as hell hope so. We've been dancing around our feelings for weeks."

"You're joking?" He leans back and crosses his arms over his chest. "You told me you love her before you told her?"

I give him a slight smile. "I've never said those words to a woman before. I came here for a pep talk."

"Here's your pep talk." He points a finger at me. "Tell her, Sebastian. Go find her and tell her how you feel."

I look down at my hands. "I'll do it tonight."

I will. Tonight I'll tell my beautiful Matilda that my heart belongs to her.

***

No. Just fuck no.

I stare down at the bouquet of flowers I'm holding.

Junior, the doorman at my building, shoved them into my hands as I was making my way to the elevator to go up to the apartment to make dinner for the woman I love.

They froze me in place.

Six black roses.

Six black fucking roses wrapped in red paper.

I look over the envelope addressed to Matilda. I don't rip it open because of the slim chance that there's a fingerprint or trace DNA evidence on it.

I already know what the message inside will read.

Detective Wolf can't save you.

The same five words were written on a card tucked into a bouquet of dyed black roses sent to my parents' apartment on Mother's Day last year.

Another was sent to my sister's store seven months ago.

"Who delivered these?" I turn to Junior. "Who?"

"I don't know." He points at the sidewalk outside the building. "It was two hours ago. I was helping Mrs. Henderson from 7A bring in her luggage. She just got back from Arizona. You'll give them to Tilly, right?"

I shake my head in frustration. "What did the person who delivered them look like?"

"I never saw them." He shrugs as he takes a measured step back. "I rode up with Mrs. Henderson to her apartment to help her with her stuff. They were on my desk when I got back."

I glance over at the reception desk. "I need the security camera footage of the lobby. Get me the footage for that block of time."

He huffs out a nervous laugh. "Those cameras are for show. The owner put them up to make the residents feel safe."

"Fuck."

"What's the problem?" His head turns toward the elevator when it dings its arrival. "Tilly will probably know who they're from. A few guys know she lives here, if you know what I mean."

"No." I inch toward him and straighten my shoulders. I know exactly what he means. Matilda had a life before me. She's been with other men. I hate it, but it's her past. It means nothing to me, but I'm not about to let this bastard speak about her with anything but respect. "What do you mean?"

His left eyelid twitches. "She likes to date, okay? She's brought a handful of guys home. Let's say she hasn't been afraid to sow her oats. I haven't noticed any new guys in weeks, but it's hard to keep track."

"Shut your mouth," I seethe. "Shut your fucking mouth."

He takes another step back, his hands shaking.

"Don't you say another word about her." I point my finger at him. "Do not speak about her or to her unless you're saying hello or goodbye. Understood?"

He nods. "Understood."

I leave him there as I turn around and walk out with the bouquet of flowers in my hand knowing that when I come back to this building my life won't be the same.

Chapter 50

Sebastian

"I did it," Matilda exclaims as I step into our apartment. "I really did it."

I know what she's talking about before the words leave her perfect pink lips. She cooked dinner for me. She fucking cooked me dinner.

I can't tell what it is, but it smells incredible.

I look over at where she's standing next to the dining room table with two wine glasses in her hands.

There's a bottle of red on the table, uncorked.

"Will you do me the pleasure of pouring our wine so I can toast to tonight?"

I stand frozen in place staring at the woman I'll never get over. I'll never forget the taste of her lips, or the softness of her every curve.

I'll hold onto the memory of her voice for as long as I live.

"Matilda." I swallow hard.

"I know, I know." She places the wine glasses down. "You got busy with a case. That's why you didn't make it home first. "

No, that's not why.

I spent three hours with my lieutenant, running over every detail of the last two times the mystery son-of-a-bitch sent roses to women I love.

Christine tried to reassure me that this time was no different than the last, or the time before that.

She assigned security details to my mom and Nyx for weeks after they received their bouquets.

Forensic tests were run on the bouquets and cards. They came up empty.

The only other alarm that was sounded was when Nyx received a series of calls at her shop from someone asking for me.

It concerned us both enough that she moved into my apartment for a month. She took my bed. I took the couch and my roommate at the time, Brad, hit on her once before she shut him down.

She moved back to her place when she got sick of me telling her everything would be okay.

I didn't believe my own words, but she did.

Christine pulled the security details eventually and even though I've always kept my guard up, I felt reassured by the silence.

Until today.

I've made too many enemies to count since I joined the force. Some are locked up on Rikers Island, others have already served their debt to society and are now out looking to even the score. A few were never convicted and I've run into them on the street.

The threats are always subtly implied.

Not one has been followed through, but that's not a gamble I'm willing to take. Not with Matilda. I won't risk her safety.

There's already a security detail on her. One of the men is sitting in a car across the street from our building.

He'll follow her to work tomorrow and when his partner takes over mid-day, he'll follow her home.

They have strict orders to stay back far enough that she doesn't notice them, but close enough that they can protect her if need be.

It's not enough for me. I want to shadow her forever, but my presence puts her in jeopardy.

"Do you like my dress?" Matilda spins in a circle and the skirt of her short black dress picks up, revealing a pair of red lace panties.

My favorite.

"It's beautiful." I exhale harshly. "We need to talk."

Her smile brightens as if it's a good thing.

"Let's sit down." She gestures toward the sofa.

I've kissed her there. I've made love to her there. I wish to fuck I would have met her anywhere but in this apartment.

This is where I fell in love with her.

I settle in next to her, leaving enough space between us that I won't be tempted to take her in my arms and never let her go.

"Are we going to talk about our feelings?" she asks in a voice that's barely more than a whisper. "If we are, can I go first?"

Christ, please. Please, don't let her say she loves me.

I can't hear those words. They will haunt me forever. They will slowly kill me.

I swallow and take a ragged breath. I promised myself I'd never to lie to her. I vowed that I would always be honest with her, but tonight I have to break that to protect her.

"I'm moving out," I say it quickly to get the words out.

Her gaze drops to my mouth as her bottom lip trembles. "What did you say?"

I fist my hand on my knee. "I need to move out, Matilda. I think it's for the best."

"The best?" she repeats back slowly. "What does that mean?"

She can't absorb what I'm saying. I've seen it over and over again in my work. People unwilling to accept what they're hearing because they are clinging to what they want to believe is true.

In those cases, it's the loss of a loved one that their heart can't grasp. For Matilda, it's the death of our love.

Tears well in the corners of her eyes. "What are you saying, Sebastian?"

I scrub my hand over my face to hold back my emotions. "This has to end."

"This?" She spits the word out. "Us?"

I hang my head as I nod. "Yes."

"I thought…" She stumbles as she gets to her feet.

I'm up too grabbing for her out of instinct, but she swats my hands away. Her breathing is labored and uneven. "I thought this was different. I thought you felt what I felt."

I did. I do. I love you, Matilda. I fucking love you.

She stands in place, her hands shaking as she clasps them together in front of her. "I thought I was different."

I'm causing her pain. I need this to be done. "I haven't changed. It's me, Matilda. I can't change. A relationship won't work in my life."

Her gaze skims my face as tears stream down her cheeks. "Are you leaving tonight?"

I look over at the open door of my bedroom. "I'll go now. I'll come back in a day or two to pick up my things."

She bites her lower lip to still it. "I'd appreciate if you would text me to tell me when. I don't want to be here when you come back."

I almost double over from the look of excruciating pain on her face. "I will."

She turns and rounds the sofa in silence before she crosses the apartment, goes into her bedroom and closes the door.

Chapter 51

Tilly

"You look sad, Tilly." Cooper touches my hands with his. "Mom looks like that when one of her pet friends from work goes to heaven. Did that happen today?"

I look into his soft blue eyes. They're the eyes of an innocent child who could never understand the debilitating pain of being dumped by the person you thought you'd spend the rest of your life with.

It's been more than a week since Sebastian told me he was moving out.

I haven't heard a word from him.

I decided that if I don't by the end of this week, I'll pack up his things and have them sent to him at work.

I closed his bedroom door the night he left and I haven't opened it since.

"Something like that, Coop." I pat the sofa next to me. "Do you want to sit down so I can read you a book?"

He bounces in place. "I'll get the one Detective Wolf gave me."

It's not the first time he's brought up Sebastian since I got here to babysit him.

As soon as I arrived, he wanted to know where his best friend was.

Carolyn expertly answered for me by telling him that Detective Wolf was working on a case and would be busy chasing bad guys for a very long time.

When Cooper went to his room to get a new toy to show me, Carolyn tugged me into a hug. I needed it more than I realized.

My phone chimes as Cooper takes off in the direction of his room for the second time tonight.

Kate: ***Meet me for a drink when you're done.***

I stare at the screen for a few seconds before I type out a reply.

Tilly: ***I'm dead tired tonight.***

Kate: ***You're not using that on me again. You've been sleeping fourteen hours a day.***

I have been. I've spent much of the past week in my bed. I've only left my apartment to go to work and to come here.

I thought spending time with Cooper while Carolyn is on a date with Darrell would help, but so far it's only reminding me of the man I love.

I respond with a few taps on my phone's screen.

Tilly: ***One drink. That's it.***

Kate: ***I'll head over to the bar across the street from Carolyn's place now. I'll be waiting for you when you're done.***

I smile for the first time in more than a week.

Tilly: ***I could be here for hours yet.***

Kate: ***The martinis will keep me company.***

***

"I feel like an idiot." I sip on the glass of soda I ordered when I got to the bar. I was tempted to go for something stronger, but I'm scared that if I start pouring alcohol down my throat, that I won't stop.

It was my go-to pain reliever after my break-up with Boyd. I won't fall into that trap again.

"Because you fell in love with him?" Kate runs her fingers over her chin. "Don't beat yourself up because you loved Sebastian."

Love. I still love him.

"It's not just that." I look around the crowded bar. It's the same bar that I was at weeks ago with Sebastian when he took a fist to his face.

It was the night of our first kiss and I could see forever in the distance.

Now, I only see loneliness and confusion.

"We were here one night." I point at the table in the corner where Sebastian and I sat. "We had our first kiss right over there."

She turns to glance over her shoulder. "Are you serious?"

"I am." I attempt a weak smile.

"I'm a horrible best friend." She pushes back her chair. "We're getting out of here. Let's go."

"No." I reach to grab her hand to still her in place. "I don't want to go."

She hesitates. "You don't have to be brave."

My gaze slides over to the bar and the same redheaded bartender that was here the night Sebastian kissed me. "I'm not brave."

"I asked you to come live with me temporarily, and you refused so you could stay in the apartment you shared with the man you love. Now, I'm telling you we should get the hell out of here and you're still in that chair."

I glance at her. I see the concern in her eyes. It's been a constant since the night Sebastian left and I called her begging her to come over.

She did. She crawled into bed next to me and held my hand while I wept through the night.

"Running away from memories only gives them more power. "I sip my soda. "I'm facing them. I have to."

She nudges her chair closer to the table. "Fine. We'll face them together."

"I did something the day before he left." I cup my hand around the soda glass.

"What did you do?"

"I tried to make his dream come true." I shake my head. "He made so many of mine come true that I wanted to make one of his a reality."

She downs what's left of the drink in her glass. "What does that mean, Tilly?"

"When we were here that night he told me that his dream was to be a prosecutor. One of his friends told me the same. He said that Sebastian talks to him about becoming a lawyer." I close my eyes briefly to ward off the regret I've been feeling for the past week.

"A lawyer? That's surprising."

I nod. "The day before he broke up with me he told me he was planning on meeting someone to talk about his future. I assumed he meant becoming a lawyer so when I went to work that day and saw the Dean of Admissions for NYU Law I thought it was fate."

"You saw who at work?"

I pinch the bridge of my nose before I go on, "Ron brought his cat into the clinic that afternoon and I thought it wouldn't hurt to mention Sebastian to him."

"Ron is the Dean of Admissions?" She stops me to clarify.

I nod. "Yes. He came in unexpectedly and I brought up Sebastian and his career and his admission years ago to NYU Law. Ron said he'd put together an admissions package and reach out to Sebastian to talk about his chances of getting accepted again in the future."

Her voice lowers. "Did Sebastian tell you he wanted to go to law school?"

I shake my head. "No. He never came right out and said it. I think that's why he left me, Kate."

"You don't know that."

I look back at the table in the corner. "Maybe it was my dream more than his. He was shot years ago. I was scared that it would happen again."

"He was shot?" She jerks her head back. "Oh my God."

"He's fine." I pat my shoulder. "He's fully recovered now, but it scared me enough that I convinced myself that he'd be happier as an attorney."

"Tilly." She reaches to cup her hands over mine. "He didn't leave you because you put in a good word at a law school he may never want to go to. If that was the issue he would have just brought it up and told you that he appreciated the effort, but he wasn't interested in that career path."

I shake my head in frustration. "You don't know that, Kate."

"I know that you told me very early on that he doesn't want a girlfriend."

I don't need the reminder. I haven't stopped thinking about that since the night he broke up with me.

"Tilly, he left you because he didn't want to be in a relationship with you."

The words sting. They sting as much as they do every time I let then trample through my thoughts.

I want there to be a logical reason for why Sebastian walked away from me. I don't want it to be because he didn't love me.

"You have to face this." She wraps her arm around my shoulder. "The sooner you do, the sooner you'll be able to move on."

She's wrong. My heart won't let me move on.

Chapter 52

Sebastian

"One more night on my sofa, Sebastian." Liam kicks my bare foot with his boot. "I'm giving you more night and then I want you out of here."

I don't open my eyes. "You said that yesterday and the day before that."

"Get up." He opens the curtains to let the early-morning light flood his living room.

I push my palms into my eye sockets. "Jesus, Liam. What the fuck is wrong with you?"

"What the fuck is wrong with me?" he repeats back. "I'm not the one wallowing in my own pity. I'm getting my ass to work and tonight I'm taking a beautiful woman to dinner."

"Don't rub it in," I growl.

"I had my doubts." I hear him walking around the sofa. "I admit I had doubts when you told me you loved Matilda, but I need to say, I have zero doubts now. You really do love this woman."

"I know that." I push myself up into a sitting position. "You don't think I spend every fucking day thinking about her?"

He sits on the edge of the coffee table.

He's dressed for work in a pair of black pants and a blue button-down shirt. I can't say the same. I'm wearing boxer briefs and nothing else.

The only clothes I have here are those that I could fit into my duffel bag. I stuffed that with more underwear, two pairs of jeans and a bunch of T-shirts before I left the apartment I shared with Matilda.

I had no idea where I'd end up that night until I called my youngest brother.

I didn't even try and keep it together. I sobbed into the phone and he told me to head over to his place.

He was waiting on the sidewalk in front of his building with open arms and a beer.

"Julian stopped by my office yesterday." He sighs. "He wanted to know what's up with you. He said you've been avoiding him."

I have no idea what Matilda has told her sister about me. I don't give two shits if Julian will never speak to me again after breaking Matilda's heart.

What I do care about is whether Matilda is all right.

"He doesn't know about Matilda." His hands dive into the front pockets of his pants when he stands. "He was saying something about inviting you two to dinner with him and Maya to talk wedding plans."

Shit. Their wedding.

I have to stand and stare at Matilda while two people we love promise to commit themselves to one another forever.

"Why wouldn't she have told him what I did?" I look up at my brother.

He shakes his head. "Because she loves you. She doesn't want to come between you and your best friend. It's the same reason she talked to the Dean of Admissions at NYU Law about you. This woman wants the best for you."

The sharp tone of his voice doesn't surprise me.

When I came home from work two days ago and showed him the envelope that had been hand-delivered to me in the squad room by Ronald Hixon, he didn't say a word for a solid ten minutes.

Once he did speak, his message was clear.

He told me I fucked up the best thing that has ever happened to me and I need to find a way to get Matilda back.

I can't do that.

I won't risk her safety for my happiness.

"What if this is tearing her up inside?" he asks as he heads toward the door of his apartment. "Have you thought about that? What if she's in as much pain as you are? Can you live with knowing you caused that?"

The questions bring me to my feet. My hand grazes the full beard on my chin. "I don't want that, but I can't keep her safe, Liam."

He turns back to look at me. "How many times was dad threatened when he was on the job? He didn't push anyone away. He held onto mom tighter. He held us closer."

I stare at him, listening to every word he's saying.

"Have you asked her where she feels safest?" He points a finger at me. "Stop making decisions for her. Tell her what's going on and let her be the one to decide if you're worth the risk."

Chapter 53

Tilly

"I hate leaving." Kate looks beyond my shoulder at my empty apartment. "Why don't you give me a few minutes alone in his bedroom? I can have everything packed up and sent to him in no time flat."

I love that she wants to protect me in that way, but it's my responsibility to take care of Sebastian's things.

I have no idea where he's staying now so an hour ago I sent him a short text message.

Tilly: ***I need to know where to send your things.***

I don't have to look at the screen of my phone to know that he hasn't replied yet. I've had the volume set to maximum since he walked out of here because I don't want to miss his call or text.

"I need to do this." I hesitate a beat before I go on, "I appreciate that you want to stay and take care of it for me, but it's part of the healing process, right? Letting go of the past."

She's been spouting helpful, and not-so-helpful, advice for days. I'm grateful for her support, but it's wearing me down.

I'm not ready to move on from Sebastian.

I don't know if I'll ever be.

All I do know is that tonight I need to clear out his bedroom. I don't want his belongings near me if he's not.

"I'm not going far." She reaches to touch my shoulder. "I'm going to have dinner at that Greek place we love. It's just a block over. I can be back here in five minutes flat."

"You can go home," I say trying to convince her that I'm fine, even though I'm not. "I'll send you a text before I go to bed."

"I'm in the mood for lamb." She smiles. "I'll be having dinner close by. If I don't hear from you before I pay the check, I promise I'll go home."

"You've been amazing through all of this." I pull her in for a quick hug. "I love you, Kate."

"I love you too," she whispers. "You'll survive this. I promise you will."

***

"You're crying." Frannie leans closer to her tablet. "Tilly, what is it? What happened?"

I look down at the paper in my hands. It's out of the view of the camera.

It was one of the last things I found in Sebastian's room. It fell out of a book. I went to pick up the novel to place it one of the cardboard boxes and it slipped from my hands. The paper floated out before the book hit the floor.

"I'm just…" my voice trails as I look at the date at the top of the paper I'm holding; the letter I'm holding.

It's dated four days before Sebastian moved in with me.

"You never call me." Frannie's voice is impatient. "You're scaring me. Are you hurt? Did something happen to Maya?"

"I'm okay," I whisper. "I haven't talked to Maya. I think she's fine."

"What do you keep looking at?" Her gaze drops even though she can only see my face and the top of my shoulders.

"Are you wearing the T-shirt Maya bought for us?"

I look down at the white T-shirt with the words '*Happy Birthday for Two'* printed on it.

I'd pulled it out of my suitcase the day after Sebastian left. I needed to feel close to the people I love even if I couldn't face any of them.

I've worn it to bed every day this week. I throw it in the washing machine every morning to get rid of the mascara stains that are left there when I cry myself to sleep.

I tilt my phone's screen down so she can see the front of the T-shirt. I leave my cut-off denim shorts and the letter in my lap out of view.

"I love that you're wearing it." She sets the tablet down. "Let me put on mine."

I sit silently while I hear the rustle of her movement around her bedroom.

She's back in front of the camera within a minute.

"We haven't worn matching clothes in years." A grin covers her mouth. "I love this. Do you know how much I love this, Tilly?"

I nod. "I'm in love, Frannie."

Her eyes instantly well with tears. "What? Tilly, you're in love? With you?"

With a man who passed the NYPD Sergeant Exam with flying colors.

With a man who tucked the letter notifying him of that in a book that he hid in a drawer under some T-shirts.

A book written by his brother and inscribed with the words, '*You'll always be my hero, Sebastian. The world needs more men like you. Nicholas*.'

"He's the bravest person I've ever met." I look at the screen. "He's the best person I've ever known."

"He sounds incredible, Tilly."

My eyes glisten with tears. "I didn't know a man like him existed."

"When do I get to meet him?" Her tears give way to a smile.

"He doesn't love me back." A sob escapes with the words. "He broke up with me last week, Fran."

Her hand jumps to her mouth. "Why would he do that?"

"I wasn't what he wanted." I rub at my forehead as my gaze falls to my bed and the blanket I'm sitting on. It's the same blanket Sebastian wrapped around his waist the night we met. "I wasn't the one for him."

"Oh my God, Tilly!" Frannie screams as she darts to her feet. "Get out of there. There's a man right behind you."

I turn and look over my shoulder at the only man I'll ever love.

He's standing in the doorway of my bedroom. His eyes immediately lock on mine.

"You're the one for me and I'm back to prove that I'm the one for you," Sebastian says hoarsely. "I love you, Matilda."

Chapter 54

Sebastian

I left the room so she can end the video call with her sister.

The world may see them as identical, but I could see immediately the differences in them.

Matilda is breathtakingly beautiful. Her sister is as well but Frannie's eyes don't share the same depth as her twin sister's.

Her voice is different as well. Matilda's soothes me. It offers me comfort.

Even with a blindfold on in a room filled with people, I would be able to tell the two of them apart.

I would know the woman I love just from the awareness that courses through my body when she's near.

I feel her now so I turn from where I'm standing in the living room.

Her eyes rake me.

I shaved before I came over here. I put on a fresh pair of jeans and a black sweater I bought this afternoon.

I wanted to make a better impression than I did the first time she found me in her living room.

"I love you, Matilda," I repeat the words I said to her just minutes ago. "I need you to know how much I love you."

I want her to rush into my arms and repeat the words back to me, but she stands her ground. "I thought we were going to tell each other how we felt that night, but you left me."

I reach out my hand to her. "Please come and sit with me. Let me explain."

She does. She doesn't touch my hand. Instead she sits on edge of the sofa. It's at least three feet from where I'm standing.

I don't complain. I lower myself onto the leather and face her. "I was scared."

Her eyes scan my face. "Scared? You? Of what?"

I like that her words are laced with disbelief. She sees me as a man who is fearless. She has no idea that I'm scared to death of losing her. The fear of that is debilitating.

"Months ago some asshole tried to intimidate me by sending my mom and my sister bouquets of roses that had been dyed black."

The pain that has been a constant on her face since I saw her in the bedroom, morphs into something else. It's confusion mixed with horror. "What? What kind of sick bastard does something like that?"

"We're still trying to figure that out." I lean my hand against the back of the sofa. "You received a similar bouquet last week, Matilda."

"No." Her head shakes. "I didn't. I didn't get anything like that."

Her gaze darts to the table in our living room where a fresh flower bouquet always is. The space is barren now. The last bouquet I placed there the day before I left is gone.

"Junior handed it to me in the lobby." I take a deep breath. "I lost all sense of control. I couldn't think straight. I took it and went back to the station."

She scratches the back of her hand. "Why didn't you tell me?"

I want to slide over so I'm sitting next to her. I want to hold her hand and quiet her anxiety. I see unease in her movements and I hear it in her voice. "I wanted to protect you."

She shifts so she's facing me. "Did you leave me because of the flowers?"

I nod sagely. "Yes, Matilda. I didn't want my presence in your life to put you at risk. I left to keep you safe."

Her bottom lip trembles. "I knew that you loved me. I could feel it."

I move quickly, dropping to my knees in front of her. "I do love you. I didn't leave because I didn't want you."

"I would have told you that we would face the threat together." Her hands slide to my shoulders. "I'm not afraid of anything if you're beside me, Sebastian. I need you to feel the same way when I'm beside you."

"I would die if anything happened to you." I cup her cheeks in my palms. "I thought if I left, the person who sent the flowers would leave you be."

"They have. "She glances at the window that overlooks the city. "I haven't gotten another flower delivery since."

It's been quiet. I've spent days investigating this. I've spoken to every person who owns an apartment on our block.

No one saw anything.

The person who dropped off the flowers didn't appear on any of the surveillance video I pulled from the buildings adjacent to ours.

I haven't given up trying to find the culprit, but I'm confident that I can keep this beautiful woman safe.

"What happens the next time you feel that I'm being threatened?"

I answer her question as honestly as I can. "I'll protect you."

"You won't make any rash decisions for me? You won't leave me because you think that's best for me?"

"I will stand beside you, confide in you and we will face the threat together, Matilda."

"Good." Her gaze returns to my face. "I would rather have one day with you than a lifetime with any other man. I love you, Sebastian."

Chapter 55

Matilda

I press my lips to his for a kiss before I pull back and look at his handsome face. "I love you."

"I need to hear you say that at least ten times every day, Matilda."

I laugh. "Does that mean you're moving back in?"

His gaze scans the three cardboard boxes I piled up in the foyer. "Are those my things?"

I nod as the corners of my lips dip into a frown. "I couldn't stand the thought of your belongings being so close to me. I wanted to sleep in your bed every night, but the pain was too much."

"You'll sleep in it with me tonight, won't you?"

"Can we talk about something first?" I sigh. "In so many ways I feel I know you better than I know myself, and in others, I feel like I'm wandering through a fog."

He takes a deep breath, pausing before he answers. "We can talk about anything you want."

"You don't want to be a lawyer, do you?"

"You spoke to Ronald Dixon about me." His eyes flick over my face. "You asked the Dean of Admissions at NYU Law to personally consider me for the program."

I manage a smile. "I thought I was helping make your dreams come true, but I know that it's not your dream anymore."

"I was touched, Matilda. I was deeply touched that you spoke to him on my behalf. No one has ever gone out of their way to do anything like that for me before."

"I believed, at the time, that I was helping you." I bow my head. "I know now that you have a new path ahead of you."

He saw the letter in my hands in the bedroom. I know that he did.

"Somewhere along the line, the drive to be the best homicide detective I could be was replaced with a need to do more."

I don't say a word. I want him to continue.

"About a year ago I was invited, by a friend, to attend the hiring ceremony for new recruits." He speaks softly. "They were all starting a new chapter in their lives. I remembered what it felt like for me the day I was hired, so I talked with a few after the ceremony and handed them my card."

"Did you hear from any of them?" I ask out of pure curiosity.

"Almost all of the recruits I offered my card to, called me." His gaze travels to his cell phone that is sitting on the coffee table. "At first, it was strictly questions. They wanted to know what to expect once they came out of the academy and then it turned into more."

"In what way?"

My question draws his heavy brows together. "They needed to talk to someone who had been there. They all have resources that are provided to them by the department, but they needed a friend who had been there and I became that to them."

"You still are, aren't you?" I reach to grab his hand.

"The woman you asked me about meeting. Her name is Hillary." He looks down to where our hands are joined. "She was responding to a break and enter when the perpetrator pulled a weapon on her."

I see the pain in his eyes. I know her experience must have taken him back to the day he was shot. "Is she all right?"

"He backed down." His shoulders drop. "It was a tough experience for her. The threat of death can break a person down."

"I can't imagine, " I respond quietly.

"Another rookie stepped into the middle of a domestic dispute and was faced with a distraught victim." His hand grips mine tighter. "He was in a tough situation and handled it well, but it was a lot to deal with."

"Is he okay?" I ask, hearing the hope in my voice.

"We meet for coffee at a diner near his place every couple of weeks to go over that day."

"Does that help him?"

He nods. "I think it does. He's been to see one of the department's therapists which has been invaluable, but sometimes all he needs is a buddy who gets what he's going through."

He makes his role in all of this sound simple and inconsequential. He's providing his colleagues with a level of support that is invaluable.

"There's a program the department runs for rookies. It pairs them up with a veteran." He kisses my knuckles, one-by-one. "You need to be a sergeant even to be considered."

I smile. "Lucky for you that you passed that sergeant test."

"I haven't been assigned anywhere yet, and likely won't be for months, but I want in on that program if it's possible. I want to work with rookies during their first days on patrol. I want to help them find their rhythm. I'd like to give them a base to build on that will carry them throughout their careers. I met with the department head last week to let him know that I'm very interested."

"If I didn't love you already, I'd fall in love with you at this moment."

"Fall into bed with me, Matilda." His lips brush against my cheek. "Let me show you how much I love you."

Chapter 56

Sebastian

"I'll never get enough of you, Matilda." I press my lips to the soft skin at the center of her back. "Your body is stunning. Everything about you is beautiful."

"You made me feel beautiful," she whispers as her eyelids flutter shut. "After you left I knew I'd never get over you."

"You never need to." I run my lips over the curve of her bare hip. "I'll be right here beside you, with you, until I take my last breath."

"You'll never leave me again." She slowly rolls onto her back.

I know what she wants.

I part her legs with my shoulders, exposing her beautiful pussy. I take a taste. "I'll never leave you again. I can't breathe without you."

Her hands fall to the top of my head.

Nothing in this world feels as good as her fingers guiding me to her pleasure.

"Make me come." Her voice is strained. "Show me how much you want me."

I do. I lick the seam of her pussy before I circle her swollen nub with my fingertip.

"This is heaven." Her whispers fill the bedroom.

No, this is.

I suck her clit between my lips and flick it over and over again with the tip of my tongue.

She comes fast and hard against my mouth, her cries bringing tears to the corners of my eyes.

I feather kisses over her face while she falls from the high.

"Fuck me." Her soft lips press against mine. "Please."

I smile. "I can't say no to that."

I move to open the nightstand, but the condoms aren't there. Shit. She must have packed them up and tossed them into one of the cardboard boxes in the foyer.

I look down at her, love reflected back to me in her vivid blue eyes. "I need to go find a condom. Don't move."

Her full lips part before she kisses me again. "Don't go. I trust you."

"I'm clean." I press my cheek to hers.

"Me too," she whispers. "I'm on birth control. It's safe."

My heart hammers against the inside of my chest. I swear to fuck she must be able to feel it against hers.

I slide into her. The feeling of her gripping my cock without any barrier draws a low growl from somewhere deep inside of me.

"I love you, Sebastian." Her tender voice quakes with the words. "I'll never stop."

"I'll never stop loving you, Matilda. Never."

***

A knock at the apartment door turns us both at the same time. I look toward the microwave. It's after midnight.

I'm immediately on high alert.

"Go into the bedroom, Matilda. Lock the door."

She starts toward the apartment door. She's dressed in nothing but a pair of black lace panties and one of my black T-shirts. It's too big for her and looks more like a mini-dress than a shirt, but I love that she wanted to wear it.

She slid it on as we were putting my belongings away. In her room; next to her things.

"I think I know who it is," she calls back over her shoulder.

Panic rushes over me and I stalk toward her, scooping her into my arms from behind before she reaches the door. "Let me check first. Please, Matilda."

She turns to face me. Realization washes over her expression. She knows that I'm thinking about the asshole that sent her the black roses. "I think it's Maya and Julian. Maya texted me earlier. She said that Frannie told her that a tall, dark and handsome man loves me."

I laugh. "What did you reply to that?"

Her lips press against my chin as her hands land on my bare chest. "I was too busy making love to that man to care about anyone else in the world."

I kiss her again. It's slow and deep. My cock aches for another taste of her. I feel it harden inside my black sweatpants.

Another series of raps from the door break our kiss.

"Who is it?" I ask as I stare into her eyes.

"It's us," Maya's voice calls back. "Tell me you two are together, Sebastian. Tell me you love my little sister."

I take Matilda's hand in mine and swing open the door. "I love this woman more than life itself and one day she's going to be my wife."

Maya throws herself into Matilda's arms with a squeal as Julian tugs me into a warm hug.

"You couldn't have done better, Sebastian." His hand pats me on the back. "I'm happy for you. I'm happy for you both."

We all move back into the apartment before I close the door.

I turn back and look at Matilda. Her smile is radiant.

"I told you that they were meant to be together." Maya wraps her arms around Julian. He tugs her into his side. "Look how perfect they are together."

"I see it, " he says before he presses a kiss to her forehead.

Matilda's hand reaches for mine and I grab it. "Thank you, Maya, for bringing this man into my life. I didn't know I could feel like this. I didn't think I'd ever be this happy."

I look down at her. "This is just the beginning, Matilda. Every day after this will be better than the one before that. I promise you that."

"I promise I'll love you forever, Sebastian."

I kiss her hand. "That's all I need. That's all I'll ever need."

Epilogue

6 Months Later

Sebastian

"You're next." Julian adjusts the black bow tie around his neck. "I know that Griffin and Piper are considering a date three months from now, so you need to plan fast, Sebastian. Make Tilly your wife now."

I dive my hand into the pocket of my black tuxedo pants. I scoop the two plain silver bands into my palm and squeeze them.

"Don't worry about who is next to take the plunge." I smile as I look him over. "Enjoy your day, Julian. Focus on Maya today."

"You really are the best man." His hands land on my shoulders. "Can you go check on my bride? Go see if Maya is all right."

I know she's fine.

I was with Matilda just ten minutes ago outside the hotel room where Maya is getting ready to marry the man she loves.

The ceremony and reception will both take place in the ballroom here at The Bishop Tribeca.

Dozens of people are already gathering, drinking champagne and taking in the massive displays of flowers that Maya and Julian ordered.

When Matilda and I walked through the space earlier, she was in awe.

She stopped to smell the fresh roses and orchids every few steps.

"I'll go check on her again." I turn to see the hotel room door open and Griffin walk in. His dark brown hair is pushed back from his forehead. His gaze is laser focused on us.

He's dressed as we both are, in tuxedos with a single red rose pinned to our lapels.

"When is this show going to start?" Griffin crosses the room to stand next to us. "You're making me look bad, Julian. How am I supposed to top this when I marry Piper?"

Julian laughs. "I wanted to give Maya the wedding of her dreams."

"You've done that." Griffin grins. "I just met her folks and her sister. They're good people."

They're amazing people.

We had dinner last night with Matilda's family. It was the first time I've seen Frannie face-to-face. I've been pulled into her video chats with Matilda on more than one occasion, including the night just a month ago that Frannie told us she was pregnant.

It was incredible to share a meal with Matilda's folks, Frannie, her husband and their daughters. We went for ice cream for dessert so Cooper Gallo could meet Jolie and Becca. Carolyn and Darrell are happy, taking their relationship one day at a time.

Tomorrow, we'll have brunch with my family. It's our regular Sunday routine when time allows.

The other constant in our lives is Kate. We've grown close the last few months. She's been a good friend to Matilda and is becoming one to me too.

"I'm going to see how Maya is doing." I pat Griffin on the back. "You stay here and watch over the groom."

"Have you and Tilly picked a date yet?" Griffin stops me with a hand to my shoulder. "I'm trying to win the sprint to the altar here. I'd like to slip a wedding band on Piper's finger before you do the same with your fiancée."

"You're still as competitive as you were in high school." I lightly smack his cheek. "Don't worry about us. Do what makes Piper happy."

He grabs my face in his hands and plants a kiss on my forehead. "I've never told you how happy I am for you, Sebby. I am."

I playfully punch him in the shoulder. "Never call me that again."

***

"Tell me that you haven't said a word, Sebastian." Matilda looks up and into my eyes.

We're standing in the corridor outside the room where Maya is gathered with her mom, her friends, Frannie, Becca and Jolie.

Matilda looks beautiful today, as she does every day.

Her hair is pinned up into a messy bun on the top of her head. Her makeup is minimal. The dress that she picked out with Maya is light blue. It floats around her knees and hugs her body in all the places I want to plant kisses.

I slide my hands into the pocket of my pants.

I palm the wedding rings in my right pocket, feeling the rough edge of diamonds. I'll hand them to Julian and Maya when they exchange vows in less than an hour.

When I close my hand around the two rings in my left pocket, I'm immediately comforted by the smoothness of them. They are plain, thin, silver bands that represent a love that will never die.

I tug my hand out and open my palm. "I haven't told a soul, Matilda."

She reaches for her ring. She slides it back onto her ring finger. "I hate that I'm not wearing it today."

I slide mine on too. "My hand feels bare."

"We'll tell them in a few days that we're married, won't we?" Her eyes lock with mine. "We'll tell everyone everything."

The story is as simple as it is complicated.

I married the love of my life a week ago on a beach in Mexico.

We took the trip to celebrate our love, our future and my appointment to the position of sergeant. I'll be working in the division I wanted with new police officers.

The day before we left, a bouquet of black roses was left on the step of the house we bought in Queens, but this time Matilda caught sight of the man who dropped them off as she was coming up the street after taking our dog, Lunar, for a walk.

She called me as she set off after him, following him as he strolled leisurely down the sidewalk completely unaware that she was behind him. Panic ran through me as I drove through the streets of the city, calling for any units close to where she was.

The asshole was apprehended. His grudge was rooted in an arrest I made of his brother a year-and-a-half ago.

Two days later as we walked in the warm sand and the sun was setting, I asked her to marry me. She accepted and after we made love that night, we decided that we didn't need anything but two simple rings and our vows.

She was stunning in a white sundress with her long hair blowing in the breeze and a single white rose in her hand. I wore a white dress shirt and dark blue pants. I had packed them hoping to wear them to take her out to a nice dinner.

Instead, I stood on the beach barefoot with the shirt untucked and my belt left on the bed at the hotel.

We'll get married again here, in a small ceremony in our backyard in a couple of months so that the people who love us can share in our happiness.

She slides the ring off and hands it to me. "Guard it with your life."

I kiss it before sliding off mine and tucking them both back in my pocket. "I only agreed to hold off on telling anyone because I know you don't want to take anything away from Maya's special day."

"I want her to have today." She wraps her arms around me. "She's waited for this day for a long time."

"I've waited for you forever," I counter with a soft kiss on her mouth.

"You have me now so never let me go."

"I won't, Mrs. Wolf." I press my lips to hers. "I'll never let you go."

Preview of SIN

A New Standalone Novel

West.

That's what he said his name was when I met him on the flight from New York City to Las Vegas.

I was on my way to sin city for a bachelorette party. West had business there.

He was wickedly handsome, demanding, and the intensity in his eyes melted me from the inside out.

I left his hotel suite before he woke up because a one-night stand is just that. It's one night of pleasure that doesn't seep into the next day.

At least that's what it's supposed to be if it doesn't go completely wrong.

I didn’t give him my real name. We never exchanged numbers.

West didn’t need any of that to find me.

All he had to do was look across a conference table in Manhattan two months later.

Out of all the advertising agencies in the city, Jeremy Weston chooses the one my father owns to work on the campaign for the launch of his company’s latest product.

I try to pretend I’m not the woman he spent a night with in Las Vegas, but my body betrays me.

Not everything that happens in Vegas stays there.

The sins of my past are proof of that.

Author's Note: This standalone novel contains a handsome stranger on an airplane, male strippers, and a HEA that will leave you breathless. Although some characters from my previous books appear in SIN, you don't have to read any of my other books to enjoy this sexy romance!

Chapter 1

Lincoln

"If this is how you dress on Monday morning, I'd love to get a glimpse of you on Saturday night."

I close my eyes even tighter. There's no way he's talking to anyone but me.

His breath inches over the skin of my neck. "Just because you can't see me, doesn't mean I can't see you."

I thought he was still fast asleep.

When I boarded the flight in New York City two hours ago, the man in the seat next to me was already belted in and silent.

It took me a few minutes to realize that his eyes were shut beneath the dark sunglasses he was wearing.

I used that to my advantage. I spent the first thirty minutes of the flight blatantly staring at him while he slept.

Broad shoulders, day-old stubble covering his jaw, brown hair that is messed up just enough to promise a sexy, bad-boy beneath the tailored suit and expensive tie.

"I'm West." His deep voice rumbles through every part of me.

If I could orgasm just from a man's voice, this would be the one.

"And you are?" he continues talking even though I'm clearly not responding to him. "You're not asleep. You can stop pretending you are."

I bite the bullet and open my eyes. I turn to look at him.

Holy hell.

I thought this man was hot when he was wearing sunglasses.

His deep brown eyes add another dimension to how devastatingly gorgeous he is.

"What's your name?" He looks into my green eyes before his gaze travels over my shoulder length brown hair.

I turn my head so I'm facing forward again. I was the odd woman out when my friends and I decided to take this trip to Las Vegas. After a quick game of rock-paper-scissors they ended up sitting next to each other in the third row.

I was stuck with this aisle seat in the first row next to this stranger.

I can't decide if that's a bad thing or a very good thing.

"We'll revisit the name issue." He slides his hand to the armrest so it's just mere inches from mine. "I need a vodka."

"It's ten in the morning."

I catch a side glimpse of him sliding up the sleeve of his suit jacket to look at a big watch. "In New York. It's three in the afternoon in London so cheers."

The flight attendant is pushing a glass of clear liquid into his hand before I can absorb what he just said.

First class definitely comes with perks.

"Can I get you anything?" She looks me over trying to hide the smirk that's tugging at her lips.

One dose of self-esteem with a chaser of courage, please.

I wish that were on the drink menu.

"She'll take one of these," West says.

"I don't day drink." I glance in his direction again.

"You're fucking kidding me." He lets out a deep laugh. "You were sober when you got dressed this morning?"

I look down at the tight white tank top, bright pink tutu and white high heels I'm wearing.

Thank God I tucked the tiara that was on my head back into my bag after my friends took their seats.

"I'm not the only one dressed like this." I jerk a thumb over my shoulder. "There are two other women on this flight dressed just like me."

The plan we hatched a week ago seemed sane at the time.

Our mutual friend, Kendra, is set to marry her fiancé is less than a month. Since we're all bridesmaids, we thought it would be fun to plan a one-night-only bachelorette party.

Unfortunately, the only night our schedules synced up was tonight.

We told the bride-to-be to meet us at the airport since her flight from Atlanta lands thirty minutes before our flight. She has no idea that we'll all be dressed in the same over-the-top outfit she wore in the pictures she posted to social media to announce her engagement.

The part of the plan was not my idea. I was outvoted. Twice.

"I don't care about them." He leans so close to me that his lips almost touch mine. "Something tells me that you're the one who is unforgettable."

Coming Soon

Preview of VERSUS

A Standalone Novel

I chose the woman I brought home with me last night for one reason and one reason only.

She looks like *her*.

It's the same with every woman I bring home with me.

They always look like *her*.

Light brown hair, sky blue eyes and a body that takes me to that place I crave. It's where I forget – *her* innocence, my cruelty, everything.

Last night was different.

This one didn't only look like *her*, she danced like *her*, spoke in a soft voice like *her,* and when she lost control on my sheets in that split second I live for, she made a sound that cracked my heart open. My heart; cold and jaded as it is, it felt a beat of something for this one.

She left before I woke up.

I need to forget about the woman from last night, just like I've forgotten every woman but the one who started me on this path to self-destruction.

I might have been able to if I wasn't standing in a crowded courtroom ready to take on the most important case of my career staring at the woman who crawled out of my arms just hours ago and into the role of opposing counsel.

I may be a high-profile lawyer, but her name is one I'd recognize anywhere.

The woman I screwed last night is the same one I screwed over in high school.

Court is now in session, and it's me versus *her*.

Chapter 1

Dylan

The world within Manhattan is its own beast. You learn that when you live here. When you claw your way around this city looking for something that's elusive.

For some, that's a job that will actually keep a roof over their heads.

For others, it's a relationship that will stand the test of time and weather the winds of change.

I have the first and no interest in the second.

My needle in the haystack is a particular type of woman.

I don't bother with blondes.

My cock has zero interest in redheads.

For me, it's all about the type of woman I see in front of me now.

Petite, light brown hair, blue eyes and a body that can move to the beat of the music.

Experience has taught me that if a woman can dance, she can fuck.

The woman I'm watching now is graceful, beautiful and within the hour will be in my bed.

I slide off the bar stool and approach her.

"I'm Dylan."

She taps her ear. "What was that?"

I lean in closer as she dances around me. "I'm Dylan, and you are?"

"Dancing." She breathes on a small laugh. "It's nice to meet you, Dylan."

"You've been watching me." I stand in place while the patrons of this club down around me, brushing against my expensive, imported suit.

She spins before she slows. "I could say the same for you."

I look down at her face.

Jesus, she's striking. Her eyes are a shade of blue, that particular shade of blue that always takes my breath away.

"We're leaving together tonight."

That cocks one of perfectly arched brows. "You're assuming that not I'm leaving with someone else."

"You're here alone." I spin when she does to catch her gaze again.

The skirt of her black dress picks up with the motion revealing a beautiful set of legs. "Maybe I like being alone."

"Not tonight." I reach for her hand.

She slows before she slides her palm against mine. "Dance with me, Dylan."

I breathe out on a heavy sigh. I haven't heard those four words in years. I haven't danced in as long.

I pull her close to me, sliding my free hand down her back. "What's your name?"

"Does it matter?" She looks up at me.

It never does.

I dance her closer to an alcove, a spot where the crowd is thin and the music quieter.

Her body follows mine instinctively, our shared movements drawing the admiring glances of others.

She's letting me lead now, but the sureness of her steps promises aggression in bed.

"We're wasting time. "

Her lips curve up into a smile. "Foreplay comes in many forms."

"Is that what this is?" I laugh. "I want to fuck you."

She presses every inch of her body against me. "You will."

My cock swells with those words. "Now."

"Patience, Dylan." Her lips brush my jawline. "I promise this will be a night you'll never forget."

Coming Soon

THANK YOU

Thank you for purchasing my book. I can't even begin to put to words what it means to me. If you enjoyed it, please remember to write a review for it. Let me know your thoughts! I want to keep my readers happy.

For more information on new series and standalones, please visit my website, www.deborahbladon.com. There are book trailers and other goodies to check out.

If you want to chat with me personally, please LIKE my page on Facebook. I love connecting with all of my readers because without you, none of this would be possible.
www.facebook.com/authordeborahbladon

Thank you, for everything.

ABOUT THE AUTHOR

Deborah Bladon has never read a romance hero she didn't like. Her love for romance novels began when she was old enough to board the bus, library card in hand to check out the newest Harlequin paperbacks. She's a Canadian by heart, and by passport, but you can often spot her in New York City sipping a latte and looking for inspiration for her next story. Manhattan is definitely her second home.

She cherishes her family and believes that each day is a gift for writing, for reading, and for loving.

19389799R00164

Printed in Great Britain
by Amazon